NINE LIES

CEECEE JAMES

For my Family

CONTENTS

BLURB

A new love interest for Laura Lee leads to a mystery she never expected.

Working at Thornberry Manor had already proven that Laura Lee had always been open to new experiences. Little did she know that her latest love interest would lead her down a path filled with unexpected mystery and intrigue.

Ethan invited Laura to join him on one of his explorations, promising her an adventure like no other. Intrigued by the prospect of unraveling secrets and uncovering hidden truths, she hesitantly agreed. Little did she know that this decision would plunge her into a web of danger and deception.

With each twist and turn, Laura's determination to solve the mystery grew stronger. Mary, along with the rest of the secret book club were all determined to unravel the truth behind the cave's dark history.

CHAPTER 1

Sunlight streamed through a pair of twelve-foot windows that I'd personally cleaned yesterday and landed on what I knew was a costly rug. It caught every piece of orange cat fur and made them glisten.

I winced. Heaven help us if Miss Janice should see this. Grabbing the lint roller from my trusty cleaning basket, I scooted across the rug and made a few gentle swipes.

Things had changed around here at the manor. Although Miss Janice still might consider Hank a bane to her existence, the cat wasn't forbidden like he once had been. In fact, I'd seen her give his cheek a little tickle when she thought no one was watching, along with a fragment from her biscuit.

But she would never accept this.

Remembering her sneaking him that crumb made me smile. Life was better than I could have ever imagined. I enjoyed the work at Thornberry Manor, a massive manor that predated my own family tree. Loved the friends I'd made here.

And best of all, I was on the brink of possibly falling in love.

Wow, those were powerful words. As I thought them, my grin probably made me look as foolish as a sappy goofball. Sobering up, I chucked the roller into the cleaning basket and reached for the feather duster. Determined to pull myself out of sappiness, I gave the bookshelf a violent sweep with the duster.

I'd never considered myself a hopeless romantic. It was strange to suspect that phrase could actually be used to describe me. Life definitely had a way of exposing new layers in one's identity.

I absolutely believed in the hopeless part. Up until now, I hadn't had too much luck in the old romance department. However, I had a feeling that things were about to take a different turn as I thought about the sweet man.

Great. I had that goofy grin on again. I dusted harder.

I'd bumped into Brandon Schubert a few months back while running an errand for Marguerite. The head housekeeper had needed something from the florist for a tea Miss Janice had hosted for something to do with the Women's Hospital Charity. I didn't know for sure, I just did as I was told.

As I rounded the corner of the busy street, I unexpectedly collided with Brandon Schubert. My flowers had flown in the air, and a box of danishes (secretively requested by Butler) nearly smashed.

Magically, he'd managed to catch them.

He stared at me with those dark handsome eyes, and, just like in the movies, the sounds of cars honking and people chatting seemed to disappear. Then he smiled, and I grinned back, possibly looking like the Cheshire Cat in my delight.

That might have been the moment I'd fallen in love.

Thornberry Manor was a little exclusive of the dating pond. About a year or so ago, I had a bit of chemistry with Stephen, the manor's gardener, but it had been going slow. I couldn't blame him because he was raising his little sister, and that was his priority. As it should be.

So, Brandon came as a complete surprise. We exchanged numbers and immediately started texting back and forth. Those chats transitioned into a couple of coffee outings. Granted the coffee dates happened during the day, and we both paid for ourselves, and maybe I was the one that invited him. But still.

So you can imagine how excited I was when, earlier this week, Brandon asked me to join him on a nature hike. He'd always been adamant about not leaving his comfort zone or taking long trips, so I was excited for an adventure. Being a fan of hiking, this was right in my wheelhouse. I even had a pink camo baseball cap and a cute set of boots.

That morning, I shared with everyone in the kitchen that I had plans to go out with Brandon. Mary and Lucy gave me their congratulations, while Marguerite reacted by rolling her eyes as she polished two crystal vases. She wasn't a fan.

"Why don't you like him?" I asked, curious. But only mildly because Marguerite was known for her displeasure at anything she thought unseemly behavior.

She narrowed her eyes, and I knew I'd be in for a story. Years ago, Marguerite had spent a bit of time as the small town's substitute teacher. As a result of her years in the formative classrooms she believed she had a handle on the pulse of everyone's character that passed through those doors. Brandon was no exception.

"That young man cheated on his test. Anyone who's willing to cheat on a pop quiz will cheat at life," she declared adamantly.

Cook snorted. "Oh, pooh, Marguerite. You're being too hard on the kid. Don't you remember puppy love?

Obviously not, because it's been so long since you've been young."

Marguerite narrowed her eyes but Cook ignored her. Instead, my defender propped her feet, clad in bright red wool socks, up on a stool and took an unconcerned sip of tea.

Marguerite lifted her chin and gave the vase an extra polish. "Like I said, he's a cheat. Let's not forget about how he speeds around in his car. Thinks he's some race car driver. I swear he will be the death of someone. Probably part of that backwoods racing that keeps happening around here. I keep telling Sheriff Jones he simply must put a stop to it."

"Racing, Marguerite?"

"That's right. It's not the brightest of hobbies when you're throwing massive machines down raggedy roads where other people are driving about."

Standing behind her, I caught Mary's wide-eyed gaze. With a sneaky grin, my friend raised her eyebrows as her left hand mimed turning a steering wheel sharply as she ran into the sink.

It's safe to say I didn't let Marguerite's opinions bother me. Brandon was sweet and funny. Besides that, people change, not that I would say as much to Marguerite.

Instead, I answered, "Thank you. I'll try to be careful."

It was true, I knew Brandon was a little bit of a lead foot and his car was old but sporty, but he had never said anything about racing, legal or not.

She shrugged. "Easy is as easy does," she said, which was her response to anything she didn't want to argue over. She had a way of ending the conversation on her terms.

So, this afternoon, I had Mary drop me off at the corner of our coffee stand. I saw him waiting for me, carrying two to-go cups of coffee.

I grinned. Already that showed a step in our relationship.

Brandon shrugged his hair off his shoulders and grinned at the sight of me. He had that kind of long hair that would never smooth into a man bun. I was happy about that, even though it snagged out in every direction, including, unbelievably a little bit on top.

"Good afternoon, Miss Laura Lee," he said and handed me the cup.

Such nice manners. "Is that for me?"

"You better believe it."

"Thank you so much." I accepted the coffee with a smile I could barely keep off my face. I tried to act smoother. "How are you?"

He reached up to press down that one piece of hair waving like a flag on top of his head. Somehow he just missed it. "I'm good."

"And how is work?"

"It's great! I have a new client. It's going to make me some money." He glanced down. "I like your boots."

I pointed a toe at him. "You told me to dress for a hike."

"You did good." His eyes lit up appreciatively.

I took a sip of the coffee. A mocha, my favorite. He remembered.

"All right. You ready? Let's go," he said.

He led me to the low profile, classic car. It was the first time he'd driven me anywhere, and I thought about what Marguerite said. Would he race this?

He even opened the door for me. Two empty coffee cups spilled out and rolled into the parking lot.

"Whoops. Sorry about that." His face flushed as he chucked them into the backseat. He waved his hand gallantly. I climbed in, and we were off.

But he didn't take me into the mountains like I expected. In fact, the hike turned out to be in a much different spot. Like, literally, it was straight off the side of the highway.

I turned to look at him, tempted to ask if he was teasing me.

He shrugged. "There's a rumor that there's a cave down there somewhere. I have to check it out, because it's got something really cool hidden in it. I overheard some guys at my new job talking about it. It's kind of a secret, all real hush-hush. I want you to come with me."

"What kind of something special?" I asked. "Treasure?"

"Maybe. Don't know." He shrugged. "That's what we're going to find out."

He climbed out of the car. Gingerly, he looked over the guard rail, which didn't inspire any confidence in me. Then he nodded and sauntered back to the car. He popped open the trunk where I saw him pull out a length of red rope. On the end was black tape with a blue star.

"What's the blue star for?" I asked.

"Put it on all my tools. Now, let's go."

He looped around the guard rail and stared back at me with a cheeky grin.

I blinked. *You're kidding me,* I thought.

Nope, he was not.

He waved encouragingly. "Are you coming or what? We've

got to get this hike over quickly. I don't want the car sitting on the side of the road for too long."

"Why?"

His brow wrinkled as he studied at his car with some concern. He checked both directions down the road. "Some people have a thing for classic cars, you know, so I've got to be careful. Come on."

All right then. Here we go. I took the last slug of my coffee and immediately regretted fueling my bladder. By the time I'd climbed out of the car, he had already disappeared.

I peered over the side. He was already halfway down the rope.

"Come on down! It's a new rope!" he encouraged as rocks bounced down past him. "Has superior tensile strength for heavy loads. Plenty strong enough."

"What? Are you poking at my weight?" I teased.

I didn't hear him answer since he was nearly at the bottom. The embankment appeared quite steep, but not so steep that I would be dangling for my life. I swung my leg over the guardrail just as a car whizzed by. The following wind pulled my hair over my face.

"Fantastic," I grumbled to myself then grabbed the rope that was supposed to be used to help me down. "Here goes nothing."

The rope steadied me as I found footholds on the way down through the muddy terrain. Honestly, I didn't need it as much as I thought. I skirted around a bush and past a sapling. A few more steps, and I ended up in a pile of bushes that probably would have originally swallowed me up. Fortunately, Brandon had trampled them down so I had a nice, soft landing pad.

"Great job," he said, his eyebrow arching in appreciation. He held out a hand to help me up.

Okay, that did feel kind of good. I didn't want to think about climbing back up though. I had a feeling that would be much more difficult.

He stooped down and picked up a rock. With a grunt, he hurled it. I heard a metallic clink.

"What was that?"

"Some stupid trail cam."

What had I gotten myself into? "A trail cam?"

"Sure. We have a lot of hunters in the area. Bears and stuff. Don't worry about it. I cracked the lens."

I shivered, more than ready to get out of here. "So where is this cave?" I asked.

"What the lady wants, the lady gets," he said, brushing back his hair and then gestured with his hand.

Hidden underneath a pile of blackberry bushes was a dark narrow entrance.

I peered at the little opening. "Is that safe?" I couldn't help asking.

"I'm here to protect you, my lady!" He gave a lavish bow, turning my frown into a giggle. "Come on." He started down the path, his boots squelching in the mud.

I followed much more carefully. By the time I made it over to the entrance, he had already peeled back a few of the larger branches. With a grunt, he hacked at the blackberries with a knife.

Finally satisfied with the opening, he pulled out a headlamp and switched it on.

"Right, let's check out this bad boy." He slid inside.

I followed. It was a dry cave, for which I was grateful. Nothing wet or murky. I ducked because the entrance was very narrow and the ceiling low. The air was musty, filled with the scent of dampness and earth. Fortunately, the deeper we crept in, the higher the roof rose above us. After about fifty feet, I could stand up. It wasn't enough for Brandon to stand. I caught him as he checked the ceiling.

"What are you looking for?" I asked. "Stalactites?"

"Bats," he answered.

My mouth went dry.

"Don't worry. We're fine." He flashed that cheerful grin.

"Now what?" I asked.

"We have to keep going," he said. "It's probably just around the bend."

"What is?"

"Come on."

We walked further. A strange smell hit me. It took a moment for me to realize it was the acrid burning odor of a cigarette. I rubbed my arms which prickled with goosebumps. What was in here? Darkness shrouded the cave, while slivers of light seeped through the crevices in the rocky walls. since the only real light came from Brandon's headlamp. I pulled out my cellphone and switched on the flashlight. Brandon glanced back to be sure I was following.

I saw footprints on the sandy cave floor and wondered about the other visitors. Recently? Weeks ago? I thought he said this cave was only a rumor?

Based on the cave's low elevation, it was clear that rainwater had seeped in, suggesting it happened after the previous heavy rainfall. My attention was caught by something vividly red, so I bent down to retrieve it. The lighter had a metallic skull sticker peeling off one side, like those metal flip lighters. With a frown, I tucked it away in my pocket. Apparently the smoker was either clumsy or didn't respect nature enough not to litter.

Suddenly, a clicking noise echoed from the depth of the cave. My muscles tightened with fear. I flashed my cellphone around, and strained my ears to figure out where the sound was coming from.

"Did you hear that?" I whispered.

"Yeah," he said quietly, stopping.

We stood there, me frozen with fear, as the sound changed. It turned into a low rumble, echoing through the cavernous space. My heart raced, pounding against my chest, my body tense and ready to react.

The next thing that happened was a boom. I clasped my hands over my ears. Brandon did the same. He pushed me with his other hand.

"Go! Go! Go!" he yelled. At least I think he yelled. My ears were ringing so bad. He shoved me back towards the entrance.

I ran, tripping over stones. Dust kicked up and then he pushed me out. Blackberry branches slapped at my face.

Out in the sunshine he looked around real quick. No one was around.

"Quick, climb up the rope," he instructed. I ran for it. Huffing loudly, he was right on my heels.

The rope creaked in my hand. I climbed the rope as fast as I could but apparently it wasn't fast enough because every now and then he would give me a boost with his head on my rear.

Finally we were over the railing, and he was pulling up the rope.

"What was that?" I asked. "An explosion?"

"It was a gunshot," he said grimly.

That coffee almost betrayed me. "Do we call the police?"

"And say what? I didn't see anyone. You didn't see anyone. There's a small chance there's somebody doing some actual hunting." He scanned through the trees again one last time and then pushed me toward the car.

"Come on. We're getting out of here," he said.

I hoped we could go someplace and at least finish our date. But he didn't seem interested anymore. He drove back to the coffee shop quiet and deep in thought.

"Are you okay?" I finally asked.

He nodded. "You have a ride?"

"Yeah, My friend, Mary. I'll call her and have her pick me up."

I was surprised and a bit hurt by his absentmindedness.

"Good, good," he said, "All right. I'll talk to you later." He gave me a weak little wave.

"Okay. Well, goodbye." I climbed out of the car. Thoroughly confused, I watched him drive away.

CHAPTER 2

*T*hat night, Brandon had been unusually quiet during our normal texting time. Disappointingly, he hadn't responded to my final goodnight message.

I checked my phone first thing in the morning, and he still hadn't responded. Slightly discouraged, as well as confused, I tucked my phone away and hurried down to the kitchen.

I'd hardly sat down for breakfast (a lovely poached egg on toast. Cook had wanted to spoil us this morning) when my cell phone rang.

It had to be Brandon! Possibly apologizing for the weird way he ended things yesterday. I fished it out of my pocket in a panic.

"Hello!"

"Is this Laura Lee?"

An unknown male was on the other end. Frowning, I answered, "Yes? This is she. I mean, me."

Cook's attention was immediately grabbed. I could see from the sparkle in her eyes that she thought something worth a bit of gossip was about to happen.

The man continued. "This is Officer Sorrento. I'm calling to find out the last time you saw Brandon Schubert."

No question on earth could have caused my muscles to freeze more tightly than that one. "Excuse me?"

"Brandon Schubert. When did you last see him?"

I swallowed hard. "Uh, I-I saw him yesterday." My words came out in a stutter. I now had Mary's attention as well, causing her fork to stop midway to her mouth.

He sounded cold and hard. I couldn't read his intentions. "I see. Could you provide me with some additional details of your last meeting?"

"Well, we visited a cave, explored a bit, heard a scary noise, and quickly left."

"What kind of noise?"

"He thought it was a gunshot," I said, but even as the word left my mouth, I wondered if he had been overreacting. This whole phone call had me discombobulated. I really couldn't think straight.

"I see." Again that dead tone. And then, "I'm sorry to tell you that Brandon has had an accident. It was a fatal one."

The world fell away from me then. I remember screaming, "Mary!"

She jumped from her chair and came running. The next moment both Cook and Mary were near me. Cook's arms held me as her hand moved to pet my hair. "Honey! Oh, honey! What's the matter? What's the matter?"

"Miss Laura Lee?" the officer continued on the phone. "Miss Laura Lee?"

I couldn't answer anymore. Feeling boneless, I slithered to the floor, wishing it could swallow me up.

Cook grabbed the phone from my hand. "Hello? Who is this? What did you say to her?" Her lips pressed tightly as the officer filled her in. "I see." She nodded solemnly, her cheeks flushed. "Well, she's answered you, then. Is there anything else you need?"

There was a pause, and then she said, "All right. I'll let her know."

She ended the call and glanced with sympathetic eyes down

at me. I could hardly bear it. Mary had scooted to sit on the floor with me.

I couldn't believe he had died. My friends held me as I sobbed.

After what seemed like an eternity, I finally started to calm down. I wiped my tears from my cheeks. "I didn't even ask how it happened. Do you know?" I glanced at Cook.

"Well, apparently my darling, he died at that same cave that you guys were at."

Horror filled me as I stared at her.

She patted my back. "There, there, honey. I'm so sorry. But those caves are very dangerous around here. You really can't be exploring them like that. I'm sorry, but that poor boy should have known that. After all, he's grown up around here. They're off-limits for a reason."

"Cook," Mary said quietly.

The poor woman sighed. "I'm sorry. I'm not trying to be uncaring. I'm just a little mad that he would do that because he knows the rules. And now we're all going to be hurting for quite some time."

I felt my lip quiver again. Cook became matter-of-fact. "Come, now. Up off the floor. Let me go get you some tea."

"When we were down in the cave, everything was fine," I said, accepting the helping hand. I settled in the chair and she bustled off for the kettle. "It was safe. Boring even. Not even a bat." My eyebrows raised. "Then we heard the gunshot. Somebody did this to him."

Mary made a soft agreement noise and handed me a box of tissues.

"Unfortunately, that's not the case, honey." Cook clinked a fresh tea cup into a saucer. She filled it with steaming water and brought it back. "They found the rope frayed in two pieces. It appears to have snapped when he was descending."

I shook my head. "No. That's not possible. There's no way. That was a brand new rope."

"Well, brand new or not, that's what they found when they saw his car parked there at the side of the road. The rope on the guard rail grabbed the police officer's attention and made him stop to investigate."

"The police found him this morning?" I stared out the window at the rising sun in confusion.

"I'm not sure. He didn't say."

"How did they know I was with him?" I asked. I went for a tissue to wipe my face again.

21

"Now that's a good question," she said. "Maybe one of his friends told him? Or they looked through his phone?"

I cringed, humiliated to think of someone reading through my messages to him.

"Thank you, ladies." I gave Cook another hug while Mary smiled sympathetically. I left for the restroom to wash my face. When I returned, Cook was popping in an English muffin in the toaster. On the table was a little honey jar with the bear scoop. I recognized it as what she used when someone was sick.

I guess grief met the bill.

I took my cup of tea and stared out the window as I sipped it. Cook and Mary both seemed content to let me have my quiet.

The toaster popped up.

I turned to them and said, "I don't know what happened, but it wasn't an accident. We went there in search of a rumored treasure. Obviously, there must have been others who were aware of its existence. I'm positive that there was another person inside the cave with us. Brandon must have gone back inside after he got me out of the area safely."

"Well, dearie, the police think this is a closed case. Open and shut, the officer said. Now we should probably get to making some things for one of us to bring over to his mother. Bertie is a good woman, and I am sure she's just devastated. Go ahead and take a little break and have a snack. I'll let Marguerite know. Mary? Can you bring the tea up to Miss Janice?"

"Of course," Mary answered, jumping up.

Cook came over with the English muffin. "Shock needs to be fed. This will help, I promise."

I nodded.

She nudged over the butter. "There now. Just a few bites. And maybe this afternoon, when you feel a bit better, you can go check in on his mom. Bring the basket from all of us. That would be nice, I think. Sound okay?"

"Yeah, okay," I said sadly.

"I'll clear it with Marguerite. We'll get something nice made. Maybe Brad can drive you."

Brad was the manor's newest chauffeur, a young man who stayed to himself. Butler scoffed in wonder if the poor man was old enough to have his license yet.

She left me to myself where I quickly ate a bite of the muffin then set it back on the plate. After a short time, I picked up my phone and headed to my room.

Hank was there, my sweet orange-marmalade cat, waiting on the bed as if he knew I'd need him. I held him like he was a warm stuffed animal and buried my face in his fur. He licked my hand and started purring, and we sank into the worn quilt that smelled like Marguerite's special lavender softener. His warmth and sweet vibrating sounds comforted me where words couldn't reach, and I silently thanked God for animals.

After a few minutes, I rolled to my side. I began scrolling through our text messages. I went back and read the last one Brandon sent me.

—That hike was pretty crazy. Thank you for coming with me

I remembered how distracted he'd been when he dropped me off at the cafe last night. Something had been up with him, and I was going to find out.

CHAPTER 3

I'd only been resting a short time when I heard a soft tap on my door. Hank gave my hand a goodbye rub before hopping off the bed. His tail flicked as he disappeared inside his little hide-away by the wainscoting. He wasn't into visitors. Unless he was; it was always up to him.

Marguerite entered. Her no-nonsense face was a bit more rigid than usual, with her mouth stiff and tight. "How are you, my dear?" she asked.

The lump immediately grew in my throat. I found myself crying once again.

She quickly bustled over and bent to give me a hug. Between

being mashed into her squishy bosom, and the firm pats on the back, she stammered out, "I heard. I heard."

I silently prayed that she wouldn't confirm her earlier, "I told you so."

But the head housekeeper did nothing like that. Instead she said, in a sweet, sympathetic voice, "We're all here for you, dear. Now, Cook says you're going to commiserate with his mom, Bertie. I know her from church and I think it's appropriate and lovely. Why don't you come with me?"

She led me downstairs and into the narrow hallway toward the butler's pantry, where the aroma of freshly baked goods filled the space. Briskly, she reached for a sturdy wicker basket from one of the upper shelves. With swift and skillful movements, she carefully filled the basket with several jars of both sweet golden honey, and fruit jam. In between these she nestled wrapped, flaky croissants, alongside a variety of delectable cookies. The clinking of glass jars and the rustling of the wicker basket brought a layer of comfort. Maybe Cook was right about feeding grief.

With a compassionate smile, she lifted the basket. "It might feel strange to give food to people who've suffered a tragedy like this, but I always feel it's like a tangible hug for when they need it." She patted my arm. "I know this will be hard for you. But I believe it will be good, as well. Now, come along."

Brad had apparently been briefed because he was standing by the town car. They piled me into the back seat with Cook pressing a real handkerchief edged in pink lace into my hands. Then he whisked me out of town. I stared out the window as my mind went over every conversation from the previous day. Little details like the swoop of Brandon's hair and his smell overwhelmed me. I felt so lost.

The drive seemed too short when we arrived at Brandon's mom's house. There was a large crowd already at the small bungalow, with a little porch filled with people who spilled out of the building. The group parted as I approached, allowing me to quietly move up the stairs. I kept my head ducked down, trying to keep a low profile.

My basket caught someone's eye, and they quickly escorted me to the kitchen. The counters were crowded with covered dishes; many, many tangible hugs. I made room for my basket on the kitchen table.

All around me people talked in hushed tones. I felt like a fish out of water, hopelessly out of place since I didn't know, anyone.

His mom sat on the couch, surrounded by sympathetic ladies. They murmured and patted and passed her tissues. The air smelled of funeral flowers.

Someone placed a gentle hand on my elbow. A woman, her hair in tight brown curls watched me solemnly. "Hello, dear. Such a terrible day. Did you know Brandon well?"

I swallowed as the lump rose in my throat. I couldn't trust my voice to answer, so just nodded.

"Such a tragedy. Just terrible," she said. Her eyes were puffy. She asked again, seemingly trying to pin me down. "Did you work with him?"

"We were friends," I answered quietly.

"Oh, dear. And when did you last see him?"

Suddenly, I realized I couldn't do this. I couldn't discuss the cave and the hopes I had with a woman I didn't know. I couldn't relive that memory here in this stranger's house.

"Will you excuse me, please?" I asked. Before she could respond, I walked over to where Brandon's mom sat.

She glanced up as I approached, her eyes red-rimmed from tears.

"Mrs. Schubert I just wanted to say I'm so sorry."

"Thank you," she whispered.

I nodded and swallowed and blinked back tears, and felt about as useless as a glass hammer to offer any comfort.

Finally, I lifted a hand in a pitiful goodbye and did an awkward few steps backwards.

Ducking my head, I ran out the door.

Brad didn't say anything as we drove away. I rolled down the window and the cool air rushed against my face. I took in a few grateful gulps.

I didn't want to go home. I didn't want to go sit and stare and drown.

"Can you drive me around a bit?" I asked the driver.

"Absolutely." He watched me in the mirror. "Do you have a particular place you want to go?"

"I just want the wind blowing and some time to zone out. Maybe some music. Just for a short bit. If that will be okay?"

His reply was to turn on the music.

For the next forty minutes, he took us down a few country roads and then out onto the highway. I found myself staring out the window, lost in surreal thoughts.

He drove down the narrow country road, the wheels humming softly against the pavement. Rays of golden sunlight filtered through the trees, casting shadows on the car's interior. My focus was more fixated on inner thoughts rather than on the scenery passing by outside the window, so I didn't notice when he seamlessly transitioned onto the bustling highway.

I quickly straightened as I realized where we were. He slowed the car at the crossroads where we could turn left and head home or right and go past the cave that Brandon and I had explored.

"Wait, stop!" I said, sitting up. "Can you turn right?"

Brad was so amazing, he didn't even question me. He just flipped on the signal and eased out into the traffic.

A few minutes later, I saw where we had climbed over the guardrail to explore the cave. It was easy to identify exactly where. Flowers and other tributes stacked up against the guard rail.

"Can you please pull over?" I asked, my mouth dry.

He did as I asked, and I climbed out of the town car. Tears poured down my face. I wished I had brought my own flowers. It was very surreal to think I was just here the other day.

I squatted down by the flowers and picked up a couple of the notes. Most of them said, "I miss you," or, "You were a good friend."

Something caught my eye on the other side of the guardrail. A blue stuffed animal had fallen over the edge. Leaning over the rail, I stretched to reach it, groaning as I realized it was just past the tips of my fingers. A quick check showed no cars coming. Brad seemed to be distracted by his phone. I hated to see the bear there, cast over the side.

I hopped over the guardrail and scooped up the teddy bear. I grabbed the guard rail and was about to climb back when I saw another one a couple feet down. I could reach, I know I could. I put the first one over the side and then carefully slid on my rear to reach the next one.

This one turned out to be a toy duck. I grabbed it and instantly feeling a shiver.

This was the place where Brandon's death most likely occurred. How could it have happened? It made no sense. Even if the rope had snapped, here I was, nearly halfway down without any rope at my disposal. The slope appeared alarmingly steep from the guard rail. But the descent proved it was manageable, especially for someone as athletic as Brandon.

I glanced around at the same undergrowth I'd seen earlier, trying to find a safe place to land. Funny how the bushes and ferns had all popped back up again, erasing the effects of human presence.

Something glistened at the bottom, peeking from beneath a pile of leaves.

I stared at the guard rail, calculating my way back. It would be hard without a rope, but not impossible. There were roots and branches to grab. I had confidence now.

"Okay, sparkling thing, show me your secrets," I said under my breath and carefully slid down the hill.

I landed in the pile of ferns. I'd lost sight of the sparkling thing. Frowning, I walked back and forth in search for it, but it had disappeared.

The cave's mouth released a rush of cold air. I took a few steps back up the hill again, clutching onto branches and ancient tree roots for support. After ten feet, I turned around and searched for it again.

There it was! A one-in-a million shot with the sun hitting it from a certain angle. I kept it in eyesight as best as possible as I slid back down.

When I reached the spot, I saw it was deep in the mouldering leaves. With strong determination to repel all thoughts about spiders or worms, I reached inside.

There was something chilly and solid. I gasped at the wet leaves but managed to pull it out.

A wooden handle, and an intriguing carving. It was a knife. Was it Brandon's? I couldn't remember. I brushed it off and held it to the sun to discover a bird that resembled a Phoenix.

There was something else on the ground. A cigarette butt in the mud. It reminded me of the smell when we had been in the cave. Wrinkling my nose, I picked it up and looked at the little label on the side. I tucked it in my pocket, along with the knife.

I walked over to the cave and peeked inside the entrance, using the light on my cell phone to see. I wasn't sure if I was brave enough to go in there by myself. However, even from the entrance, I could see a lot of people had been in there since the other day. Footprints were everywhere.

Somehow that made the place less scary to me, but also less special to know that everybody had been tramping where we had our first date.

I took a deep breath. "Brandon, I miss you," I whispered, my eyes burning.

"He misses you, too," someone said. I jumped like a mile. Another woman came around the corner, her hair in two braids.

"Who are you?" I asked.

"I'm Brandon's aunt, Irene."

I wanted to ask what she was doing there but she could easily ask me the same thing.

"I saw some stuffed animals had fallen down in and went to get them." I plucked the duck out of my pocket to show her. "I just wanted to come and pay my respects and let him know I missed him. Then I saw these had fallen." I saw a pained expression cross her face. "I'm so sorry." I blurted out.

"I liked your first question. You've got gumption, also shows you're thinking like me. What was your name?"

I gave it.

"Laura Lee." She rolled it over her tongue. "You're that young girl that he was seeing, is that right? He said he made a new friend."

I wasn't sure if I enjoyed being described that way, but I nodded.

"Well, Laura Lee, I can tell you that my nephew did not die by having the rope break. Somebody's giving us so much malarkey, and I need to find out who and why."

"How do you know?" I asked even though I had thought the same thing.

"Well, you came down just fine without a rope, right?"

"Yes. I thought that myself," I admitted.

"So did I. Furthermore, what could have led to the rope breaking? Did you happen to see any rope shreds on that guard rail? Because I sure didn't."

"Very good point," I said.

"I mean what would he tie it to? His car?"

"We tied it to the guardrail," I said.

"We?"

"Brandon brought me here, yesterday. He had heard some rumor or something about a treasure," I smiled. "You know how boys can be about adventures and treasure?"

Irene laughed. "That sounds like Brandon. What a date! Did you find it?"

"No, that's the weird part. We got down here and went inside, but we heard a noise, like a gunshot or something, so we quickly left."

"I see."

"I was just thinking about going inside to see if I could find what he was looking for."

"Let's go."

We followed our old footprints into the cave as far as they went and continued on. Our path ended at a rock wall.

"This is it," I said, disappointed. The cave had a back and didn't go any further. Brandon had died for nothing. There wasn't even a spot to hide anything in the cave.

"He was wrong, I guess."

We walked back out of the cave into the fresh air.

My heart felt heavy with confusion. "He had a look in his eyes though, you know, all distracted looking. I should have known he would come back."

"It isn't your fault. You're too smart to go that direction with your thinking," she said sternly. I saw some of the similarities to her and Marguerite. I wonder if they knew each other very well. "Be careful," she said as she walked away.

I had a feeling she knew I wasn't going to let this go. I couldn't.

I climbed back up and found the Town car. Brad stood at the guardrail, looking down nervously. He helped me over the rail.

"My word, you scared me bad, Laura Lee."

"I'm sorry. I should have told you. I guess I just needed to say goodbye."

He nodded, but no longer looked as understanding. Brusquely, he held open the door. I climbed in, where he drove us straight back to the manor, obviously not in a mood for any more funny business.

All I could think about was the red rope.

CHAPTER 4

I walked through the back door and straight into the most delectable scent of freshly made jam. Cook stood at the counter, carefully spooning the vibrant, sticky concoction into small, glass jars. The sound of the metal spoon clinking against the glass echoed through the room, as rays of sunlight danced off the shiny surfaces of the jars.

"Jelly?" I asked, somewhat surprised.

"It's for the hospital charity auction. Miss Janice signed us up for a donation." Her pale eyebrows lifted, and she gave me a hangdog stare to show me exactly who the "us" referred to.

"Well, it smells amazing. Someone will be getting quite the treat."

"Anything for charity," she said, the little wrinkle between her eyebrows tightening as she concentrated. She finished filling the last jar and turned to me. "Now how was the visit, Laura Lee? How is poor Bertie?" Her bright eyes glanced up.

"She was very broken hearted, but also well supported. I think half her neighborhood was inside."

"Were you able to convey our condolences?"

"I tried. I almost couldn't talk at all, and I didn't want to say the wrong thing. I just can't get my head into the game."

"Poor thing. You go run to your room, take a minute and wash your face. Hurry before Miss Janice sees you."

"Oh. Does she know?"

"She knows what she should, which isn't much." Her raised eyebrows and the dip of her chin reminded me that no one wanted to bring drama to the manor, if possible.

I took her advice and flew up the polished stairwell. I washed my hands, stained green from grabbing the weeds down the hill. Then I splashed my face and dabbed on some lotion. It stung on the chapped skin. Fanning my cheeks, I searched for a clean uniform and slipped it on. After a quick brush of my hair, I ran downstairs to help out with dinner.

It was when I had a covered silver tureen in my hands, on my way to the dining room, that I bumped into Butler.

In his black uniform, he always reminded me of one of those old fashioned light poles. Tall and skinny. He asked solemnly, "I'm so sorry to hear about Brandon. How are you? I heard the funeral is soon."

"Thank you." I confessed, "I'm super nervous to go. Especially alone."

He nodded sympathetically and started to reach to touch my arm. He immediately withdrew as Mary walked by.

"Going alone? What am I? Chopped liver?" she asked.

"Of course not, Mary." I didn't know how to tell her I would feel uncomfortable and lonely no matter who came with me. In response, she gave me a sad smile and shook her head in understanding.

"Tonight, I'll make us a snack, and we'll talk all about it. Are you up for it?"

"Maybe. What are you making?" I asked.

"Cheddar cheese and marshmallows on saltines. Tastes amazing and is full of protein and carbs. It's a treat."

"That is certainly interesting," I said.

I caught Butler's nod, this time to encourage me to present the dinner dish.

I walked into the small dining room with my tureen. With professional stealth, I approached Miss Janice's left side and offered the platter.

"My, that smells good." She sniffed appreciatively, her small nose wrinkling. "What is it?"

I lifted the metal lid. "Lamb with rosemary potatoes."

She leaned forward to inspect the dish that glowed by candlelight. "Looks delicious!"

I bowed my head before hurrying back to the kitchen. Janet washed piles of dishes as Cook worked on the dessert. Jelly jars glittered like jewels along the back of the counter.

Quickly, I grabbed a towel to help.

"Thank you," Lucy said, gratefully. Her thin face was pale from fatigue. "I've been thinking about you all day. How are you doing?"

I shrugged in response and accept a wet pan. "Has it been busy here?"

"Crazy all day. Did they talk about what happened to him at the house?" she asked.

I shook my head. "I overheard a few saying the police believe his climbing rope snapped when he was trying to get down to the same cave he'd showed me yesterday."

"But you think they're wrong?"

I nodded. "Yeah, it just doesn't add up. Like the slope is steep, thats true. The rope made it easier to climb up and down but isn't really necessary. Not to mention I know he had a new rope, so I don't understand how it would have snapped."

I paused for a second, and delayed taking the cup from Lucy. "Then there was the scare."

"What scare?"

"We didn't explore the cave very much because we heard what I'm almost certain was a gunshot. We had to get out of there. Brandon was absolutely convinced there was some secret treasure or something there."

"Oh, wow!" She dragged the last word. "You didn't see or hear anything else?"

"No. However, I did find this there today."

I fished inside my pocket and showed her the knife. Quietly, I explained that I wasn't sure if it was actually Brandon's or not.

"Did you look up the symbol? Someone with experience engraving must have done it."

"What engraving?" Mary asked, entering the kitchen.

I quickly explained as I continued drying dishes.

43

"It looks hand-made. I bet we could track down where that was made."

I looked up at them. "You think I should?"

"If I died in a mysterious circumstance, I'd want someone to look into it. And I'm here to help you."

"I'm with you, as well," Lucy said.

And so it was settled. My friends would help me try to find out what happened to Brandon.

CHAPTER 5

*I*t was late by the time I was finally off for the night. It took me a bit longer than usual because I did the last load of laundry for Lucy since she'd covered for me today.

The soft glow of candlelight flickered against my bedroom walls when I entered. Mary and Jane waited there, all relaxed while sitting cross-legged on my bed with Hank between them.

A plate of unidentifiable treats sat on the dresser. Mary's marshmallow cracker weirdness, I assumed. The sweet aroma wafted through the air, mingling with the comforting scent of hot cocoa. Mary smiled and held out a steaming mug, its contents swirling with steam, while Jane carefully balanced two other mugs on her leg with two awkward clinking sounds of ceramic.

"You finally done?" Mary asked.

"More sheets than I thought possible. Though working here has taught me how to fold the bottom sheet."

"It's a skill not acknowledged enough," Mary said.

"It should be in the Olympics," Jane added.

I settled onto the softness of my bed with a sigh of relief. Part of me wished I was alone so I could pull the covers over my head and make this day disappear.

Instead, I took a sip of cocoa and smiled appreciatively. "Very good," I said. I reached into my pocket and brought out the mysterious object I had discovered earlier. Anticipation filled the room.

"Check this out." I held the knife in the palm of my hand. It rolled to the side.

"Interesting. Where did you find this?" Jane asked, setting down her cracker to take the knife.

I described my trip down the embankment.

"Wow!" she said. "You're so brave."

Mary carefully placed it on the quilt. Screwing her face up, she fished out her phone. With a subtle click she snapped a picture. "You see that tiny thing? Right there. I think that's the emblem of who designed it."

Jane leaned down to give it a closer examination. "That swirl inside a square? I swear I've seen it before. Out towards that little town, Ricksville. There's a knife shop there." She caught us staring at her. The town was pretty remote, so of course there had to be a story of how she knew about a knife shop. "What? I went out there with my dad a couple of years ago. He wanted a specific fishing knife for Father's Day so I got it for him. I wonder if the shop is still there."

I was Googling before she finished speaking. Unfortunately, nothing showed up online. Instead of being disappointed, Jane suggested that maybe it was par for the course for a small shop like that.

She added, "Maybe we should have a little road trip."

Mary beamed, always up for an adventure. "Tomorrow during lunch break. Let's do it."

We did just that the next day, taking Mary's little car. Unfortunately, Marguerite needed Jane at the last minute, which was a bummer. Jane gave us the general direction, which Mary typed it into the GPS, and we were off.

It took us about thirty minutes to find the bladesmith, which wasn't bad since we got turned around twice. The weathered, rustic A-frame wooden structure hinted at its original purpose as a house. A rough dirt parking lot sprawled before us, devoid of any designated parking lines. Mary parked where the dusty earth merged seamlessly with the lush, swaying tall grass.

Shielding my eyes from the sun, I stepped out of the car, the warmth of the day enveloping me. I felt for my sunglasses in my purse as the unmistakable scent of aged wood wafted through the air.

The front door was adorned with large, unevenly carved letters that proudly proclaimed, "Custom knives made here."

Mary stared at the building with her perfectly-plucked eyebrows raised in a, "Are we really going in there?" expression. I knew she'd stay with me.

"Okay, here we go," I said, as a way of a confidence booster. And I opened the door.

The interior of the building was spooky and dimly lit. I knew I should expect it in a make-shift building like this, but it had murderer written all over it. The walls were covered with numerous bladed weapons, while mounted animal heads, dusty and faded posters about hunting, and creepy slogans about being a knife aficionado crowded the spaces in between. Two fluorescent, rectangular lights emitted different hues and did their best to illuminate the room..

Of course, there was no one around to talk with.

"Hello?" I called. I was half-afraid to hear an answer.

Something clattered in the back. Mary jumped next to me and gripped my arm.

"Let me check," I said. I felt like the bravest woman in the world as I peeked through the open doorway.

A man sat at a bench in the middle of making who-knows-what, sparks flying. I assumed it was a knife. His thick beard covered his face, and he was dressed in a plaid button-down jacket. Long graying hair hung down to the middle of his back. He wore a worn-out leather cowboy hat on his head, while his lip bulged with a pinch of chewing tobacco.

I said "Hi, there," with as much sweetness as I could muster. After all, I was invading his workspace.

"Afternoon. Help you?" He went straight to the point.

I swallowed. "I found this little knife the other day and wondered if you could help me find out who it belongs to? It looks like it has a custom mark." A simple request, I thought.

"Bring it on over here."

I did as he asked, and he looked at it for a moment, then took it in his hand. With a frown, he opened it to test the blade on a piece of wood. My hope rose. Then he handed it back.

"Don't know nothing about it," he said, and brought up a cup to spit in.

I raised my eyebrows. "Really? The emblem is yours though, right?'

"Yeah?"

"I thought for sure I would get some answers. I showed it to this guy name Marko, and he told me to come here." Of course, I made that last bit up, to give myself leverage. I was rather proud of myself for the quick fake name.

"I said, I don't know a thing about it." His eyebrows bushed over his eyes.

I swallowed. "Do you know of a place that could help with something like this?"

"Don't know nothing about nothing." He pressed his lips together.

I chose to persist for a moment, recognizing the potential for a different answer. "Do you know something for twenty bucks?" I asked in a bit of a wheedle as I reached into my purse.

He stared at me before his gaze flicked toward my hand like I was about to offer him a dead rat. "There's nothing I can help you with. Now will you let me get back to my job?"

His bitter tone made me afraid to press anymore. Mary gently touched my elbow, obviously feeling the same way.

"Okay, thank you," I murmured.

Mary beat me to the exit. We left in a hurry.

I turned for one last look as we made for the car. It was at that moment that I spotted a tiny shop located at the end of the lot. The sound of buzzing machinery was intriguing, so I had to investigate.

The little building was as opposite as the knife shop as could be, positively aglow with little lights like a happy Christmas tree. These accentuated knives, pocket watches, wooden signs, and other items. Jim, the Engraver, the door sign said.

Mary nodded toward the back where we discovered a man in the left corner. A younger man stood before a wood table to skillfully carve a bear out of a block of wood. He gave us a cheerful smile as we approached.

"Welcome!" he said, enthusiastically.

I noticed his gaze lasted a beat longer on Mary. She always caught the attention.

"Hello, there," I smiled back. "I was just next-door trying to figure out if the guy knew who might have owned this knife. Since there's an engraving, I thought it would be smart to check in with you as well. Can I show you?"

His spine straightened, and his friendly gaze fell off. "You already talked with Clint?"

I hesitated, which he took as a yes. He blew off a bit of sawdust before saying, "Sorry, I have nothing to tell you. That's what you buy when you buy a knife like that from him. Silence."

"Oh. I see," My hand with the knife dropped slowly to my side. Then I raised it forward again. "Does this look familiar like it could've been purchased through him?"

He glanced at it and shrugged. "Yeah maybe. It's possible I saw one like that being made."

"Do you know who it was for?"

"No, I do not." He grabbed his chisel and started working again.

I tried my second option of, "How about for twenty bucks?"

He replied with a slight smile. "For twenty bucks I might have something."

Relief hit me. I was a bit worried that twenty bucks had been too cheap of a deal. "That's fantastic!" I pulled out a twenty-dollar bill (my last one) and slid it across the table's smooth surface.

He carefully stowed it away in his front pocket. "I have a vague memory of the day the knife was being picked up. A person arrived in a car that was blue."

"A blue car?" Mary asked, one eye narrowing. I appreciated her question. That had to be about as generic of a clue as one could get. I had higher hopes for that twenty.

"Yes. A blue fast one that spun out when he left. Kicked tons of dust up right when I was in the middle of trying to finish a table. Like one of those back road race cars but an old style."

"That doesn't sound good," I commiserated. "Was there anything else?"

At that question, his tone got gruff. "I said I can't help you."

I was taken back by his sudden roughness. "I'm sorry I just thought I'd ask," I said. I turned around and saw the knife maker standing behind me. Instantly, I understood, and frustration flooded through me.

"Why are you guys so tight-lipped? Neither one of y'all see anything but could really help me out." I thought that the automatic tears that beaded my eyes should have given them a boost of sympathy.

"Like I said, I don't know nothing about nothing."

I wanted to argue, but he turned away from me.

"Thank you for your time," Mary said and guided me out. Probably for the best, since my anger was about to make me say something I'd regret.

CHAPTER 6

$\mathcal{M}$ary's face was stoic (frizzy hair aside) as she stared out the windshield at the building. Clint stomped back to his shop "Well, that was certainly interesting."

I stared at the tiny knife. "Interesting is one way to describe it," I agreed. "And how suspicious is it that they don't want to even admit if the knife was made by them?"

Mary shrugged. "What do you want to do now?"

I rolled the knife back-and-forth on my palm and pondered the question. I knew we had to get back to the manor soon, but I didn't want to give up just yet.

While we sat there, the back door to the small building opened and the engraver stepped out. He lit a cigarette.

Casually, he blew out a long cloud when he saw us still sitting there. A mix of curiosity and suspicion flickered in his gaze.

Then maybe a glimmer of humanity sparked in him because he sauntered over . He leaned down to the window, bringing a heavy scent of cigarette smoke with him.

My inner voice warned, Do not make a face at the odor. It will not bode well when you need information from him.

He squinted as he took another drag off the cigarette. The ember flamed red. There was an awkward pause I had to endure. Then he said, "The thing is, I could get into trouble for saying anything."

I nodded eagerly. "I don't want to get you or anyone else into any trouble. I'm simply trying to identify whether someone I know owned the knife or not.

"You should know that a professional that works with any type of weapon doesn't exactly want to be connected to any type of crime, you get that?" he said.

"Of course. I understand. It's important to me for personal reasons."

He raised a skeptical eyebrow.

"He was a good friend of mine."

"Not so good that you don't recognize the knife."

I felt my cheeks heat.

Luckily, Mary stuck up for me then. "Please, if you can just help us. My friend is grieving here."

That spark of humanity took over for him again. He answered softly, "Look, we made a few of them. That carving was some little logo for a racing club."

"Racing?" I repeated. Here it was again, that same term. "You think that person could be Brandon Schubert?"

"Maybe. Sounds familiar."

"And he was into racing?"

"Sure. Racing. Nothing big. Back road local stuff." He stepped away from the car and took a drag on his cigarette. "There's a rumor going around that Brandon lost a bet or something."

"So you do know him."

He shrugged.

"What about the blue car?" I asked.

His gaze shifted towards the building, leading me to believe he was making sure the other guy wasn't coming out. "The owner is a fan of zooming around, but you won't catch it on the main town road too often because it doesn't meet street legal requirements. I'll tell you this, Brandon hated it."

"How do you know that?"

"We'd see it around here or there. He always glared at it like he had a serious bone to pick with whoever was driving it."

"Where did you two see it?"

"Places where we like to hang out on a Saturday night." He spit and looked away from us.

I tried one more time. "But you don't know who owns the car?"

"No, and even if I did I probably wouldn't say. Some things in these parts need to be left alone, especially by two young women like yourselves. Just be careful if you keep snooping around."

He walked off, pausing to toss his cigarette butt in a metal can before going inside.

"Thank you," I called after him, gratefully. Of course, he didn't answer. I turned to Mary. "And thank you. I was starting to lose it there for a second."

"Of course, my friend. I guess sitting around undecided can sometimes be a good thing." Mary laughed.

I smiled in agreement. "At least I have my answer."

"Alright, so now what?" she asked.

"Let's get something to eat. I know I need to even if I don't want to."

She agreed and pulled out of the dusty little parking lot and headed toward the center of the tiny town.

We passed Brandon's mom's house. I thought about the balloons and the card and felt my heart squeeze. I couldn't offer any words of comfort, but I was determined to uncover the truth about her son.

"Oh man, that jam Cook made was so divine!" Mary said, pulling me from my thoughts. "I hope she doesn't give it all away to the charity."

I nodded. All of a sudden grief hit me again. I was starting to feel very alone. Nothing seemed to matter.

"What do you think about tacos? I'm actually starving. I could totally go for one or three," she said, nodding toward a small Mexican restaurant ahead.

We still hadn't had lunch, so it made sense. "That'll work."

Mary pulled into the taco stand. As we stepped out of the car, the sizzle and crackle of the taco stand's open flames reached our ears, mingling with the lively chatter of customers seated at the outdoor courtyard. But when I smelled the tantalizing aroma of grilled meat, I practically ran up to the stand.

The waitress was a young teen who barely looked old enough to legally work. She tossed her blond ponytail off her shoulder as she came to greet us. "Tables are all full out here. Do you want to do take-out or sit inside?"

Maybe some quiet would help. "Let's sit for a minute while we think of what to do next." I replied.

"You got it," she said. With quick steps in black converse sneakers, she guided us to a booth located between the front and kitchen doors. I'd prefer to be by the window, but, since we were the only inside guests, I guess it made sense for us to be in a convenient location.

We sat down while she went to get us some water. "You remember me telling you about Millie? My cop friend?" Mary said.

I nodded. "The one you said you dated her brother?"

"Yep, that's the one. We should try to get in touch with her. She might have more information."

I eyed the phone in her hand. "You think she'd want to meet with us?"

"I mean, we're here for tacos. If anyone wanted me to talk, tacos would definitely be the way to do it."

When the gal approached with our water, I ordered a large platter of spicy tacos. Mary picked up her phone to bribe her dispatch friend.

Fingers crossed she'd come.

CHAPTER 7

*M*illie must have been free because she answered right away. Mary gave a cheerful, "Hi, Millie!" Her smile must have come through her voice, because I heard a happy answer on the other end, "Mary! So good to hear from you."

"Too long. It's been a hot minute since we last talked."

"That's right, it has. In fact, I seem to remember the last time you and the ol' bro wanted to get out of a ticket. I nearly got fired."

"Oh, that." Mary blushed at the mention of her ex-boyfriend. "Water under the bridge, and all that. So, what are you doing right now?"

"Just about to sit down for lunch. Why?"

"You want to meet me and my friend at the Taco Loco stand? I'm buying."

"Taco Loco?I Really?" she replied with what might have been a hint of suspicion.

"Sure, why not? The sun's out, and it's been forever. Besides, who would say no to tacos?"

"It's not about another ticket, is it?"

Mary laughed. "No, not at all. When can you be here?"

Apparently, there were no hard feelings over the ticket, because she agreed to meet us. Our drinks and a large platter of steaming beef, cheese, salsa filled tacos were quickly served. Mary let the waitress know that our friend was on the way so she could prepare her drink order. We each started piling food onto our plates, while going over the details of the weird engraver guy.

I'd just ended with the comment, "It feels like everyone has been lying to us," when Millie arrived.

She walked through the front door, wincing at the sudden change of lighting. Mary waved and pointed at the taco pile.

Smiling, she headed our way.

"We already started without you, but there's tons left. And

we ordered you a pink lemonade. I remembered how you liked them."

"Thanks. Sounds good, especially since someone burned popcorn in the microwave at the precinct. And let me tell you, that scent sticks with a person." She wrinkled her nose in a face to let us know exactly what she was thinking.

"This is Laura Lee." A piece of lettuce flew in my direction at Mary's gesture.

"Laura Lee, nice to meet you." She smiled sympathetically. "How are you?"

Of course she'd heard, especially since they'd called me that morning. I carefully bit the taco, leaning over to try to not spill it on my lap. "I'm trying to deal with everything. Hard to believe bad things can happen on a hike in the woods."

"You know bad things can happen anywhere," she said.

"I know. It's true."

"Have you heard anything more about what happened to Brandon?" Mary asked.

"Not since this morning," she said, picking up a taco. "Pretty much they're running a pathology panel on him just to be sure that he was sober."

I flinched. I couldn't help it.

She noticed and added softly. "Sorry, Laura Lee. It's really standard in cases like this. Other than that, there's nothing else to report. Unfortunately, I believe it's probably gonna be ruled an accident."

I nodded even as my heart sank a little. "I have a question." I wasn't sure how to ask so I fell into the hem-and-haw method. "I heard of a blue car zipping around lately that might be linked to Bobby. Do you know of one?"

She laughed. "Zippy, that's a term. Yeah, I know of it. I bet a lot of people know the blue zippy car around here."

"Oh, really? Who does it belong to?" I asked as innocently as possible and crunched in a taco.

"You know I can't tell you that." She narrowed her eyes at me.

"I'm sorry. I just got tailgated by him a few times. Brandon didn't seem to like him." I pulled the truth a little bit, but I had to know who this guy was.

"That sounds like him. Interestingly enough, he did just get a ticket."

"Oh? Does he get a lot of those?" I asked.

She nodded and popped the last bite of the taco in her mouth. She wasn't lying. She had been hungry.

"I bet his insurance is through the roof," I said. "Where did he get a ticket at?"

"It was at the Dairy Freeze intersection."

Goosebumps rose on my arms. That sweet restaurant happened to be on the same side of town as the cave. Was it possible that he'd been speeding away from the crime scene?

Mary kept quiet through all of this, concentrating on her tacos. I noticed she'd already started her fourth.

"They make them so good here," she said as she squeezed on some hot sauce.

I continued to Millie. "What day did the ticket happen on?" I asked, my hand up to my mouth to try and hide my crunching.

Her eyebrow raised. "Now, that is an interesting question. The day Brandon died."

"So, could he be a suspect?" Again, I brought out my innocent look.

"Why? He wasn't at the scene. In fact, there isn't any proof anyone was there."

"Maybe he was leaving the scene at the cave." I said.

"I hate to say this, but remember the frayed rope? We have evidence the rope broke and caused him to fall and hit his head on the rock. An accident that was both unfortunate and unexpected."

I couldn't help shaking my head. "I saw that rope. Brandon said the rope was brand new. And it sure looked like that to me."

"Brand new? I'm not sure about that."

"Maybe it was cut. Besides that it didn't seem steep enough for a deadly fall." I added.

"Height doesn't matter if you hit a rock hard enough."

I put down my taco, feeling faint, but she was focused on eating and didn't notice. "Not to mention a cut rope looks different than one that was rubbed or frayed."

"The rope we used was red and more than strong enough. He said it had a certain poundage, and I teased him that he was poking at my weight."

"Red?" Now her eyebrows lifted.

"Yeah. You couldn't miss it. That's why I figured the cops would have seen it was too new to just snap."

"I see. I'm not sure the color. I can ask."

I sat up straight. That could be it. Proof someone set up a scene. "Please let them know. I think someone faked the accident."

"I will. Just...don't get too worked up or hopeful. There isn't any evidence to suggest more than a tragic accident at this point."

"And will you talk to me about it?"

Now she had a wicked twinkle in her eye. "Maybe. I like doughnuts from Shelbies."

I couldn't help but laugh. "I guess the key to your heart is through your stomach, right?"

She seized the remaining taco. "You're absolutely right about that."

Mary nodded approvingly. "This is why we're kindred spirits. Now can't you give us one tiny hint about the owner of the blue car?"

Millie rolled her eyes. "Highland Car Repair. And that's all I'm going to say. You two stay out of trouble."

"We will!" Mary promised.

"Good, because I'm not bailing you out again."

CHAPTER 8

e could barely contain our excitement as we headed back to Thornberry Manor. Mary turned out to be quite the speedster herself. The telephone poles flew by on the roadside as I did a quick online search for the repair shop.

And hopefully avoid getting carsick.

The results were exciting. "You'll never believe this, but that garage is on our way back!"

"No way! That's perfect! We going to check it out?" Mary asked.

Her question wasn't a real inquiry, but more of an assumption. Still, I had to think for a second. "Maybe I should call Marguerite first."

"You can if you want but you know what that famous saying is."

"What's that?"

"It's always easier to ask for forgiveness than permission." She delivered this platitude with a sassy swipe of her hair.

I grinned at her. "Maybe next time. I'd feel guilty if I didn't ask. She's already been so good to me."

Cook picked up my phone call, her voice slightly impatient and huffy. I imagined I'd just disturbed her from a hard task. "Thornberry Manor. How can I help you?"

"Hi, Cook. It's Laura Lee. I wanted to check with Marguerite to see if we might take a bit longer to return."

"You need more time?" She chuckled. "One of those business lunches, eh?"

"Well, we are still tracking down some answers."

"Oh, for one of my secret book club members, I say you two go ahead and take your business lunch."

"But Marguerite—"

"She's not here. I am. And I guess I can give you permission just the same as her." A bit softer she added, "You take your time, dear. You deserve it. Now I have to get back to my bread dough. It's not very forgiving." With that, she hung up.

"Well?" Mary asked.

"We're good to go." I glanced back at the map. "Now you have to take the next left." I read the descriptive blurb that came along side the garage address. "Interesting, it only got three stars."

"Okay, then."

We drove off the main road and into the boonies. Then the pavement abruptly stopped and a rough dirt road began, complete with potholes. After about ten minutes of joggling about, I started to feel nervous. Mary must have felt the same, judging from the way she gripped the steering wheel.

"You sure this is the right way?" she asked.

"Map says we're coming up to it," I said, glancing back at the phone.

Soon after, the navigator announced that we had arrived. Mary slowed as we looked. It wasn't very encouraging since nothing appeared different. Just more of the same bushes and trees along each side of the dirt road.

Then I spotted a gap in the undergrowth. But, we'd passed it before I had time to comment.

But not before I spotted something blue.

"That was it. I think maybe I saw a blue car there up on the car lift."

She gasped. "What do you think? Is this the guy who raced Brandon?"

"I think I need to have an excuse to go talk to him. Maybe we should go in. I'll make an excuse about pricing an oil change."

It was a super humid day, and I was already sweating. Plus I'd spilled some salsa on my shirt so I felt like an onion. Not to mention the heat had turned my clothes into what felt like plastic wrap, which was not my best look.

Mary did a U-turn, driving partially on the shoulder. The next minute, we were nosing down the driveway and into the dusty parking lot.

The garage stood amidst a tangle of overgrown weeds, its weathered walls and crumbling roof telling tales of neglect. Vines covered the rough texture of the siding.

Mary rolled down the window and chirping insects filled the silence. "Let's just check it out before we commit," she suggested.

"I agree."

A mechanic suddenly appeared from under the car. He had on gray overalls with greasy streaks on his cheeks. Just as intriguing, he sported a cauliflower ear. The weird bubbly scarring was common in people who took severe blows to the ear. A fighter, maybe.

And it certainly couldn't be missed. He had worked a gold hoop through it to draw the eye's attention even more.

We both got out of the car while I bit my lip to resist saying "Arrrr," to him in my best pirate accent. *Don't do it, Laura Lee.* Coming off as a loon would probably not be my best introduction.

"Hello," I said, as the scent of gasoline and rubber filled my nostrils. We walked up to the open bay. "We heard about this place and wanted to see the cost of an oil change."

"Oil change?" He sneered. "Why don't you go down the street to Jack's. That's all they do down there."

This was not going well. "Our friend asked us to get this car serviced and recommended you to me."

"Who was that?" he asked. His eyes tightened with suspicion.

In my panic, I nearly mentioned Brandon. *Be cool,* I warned myself.

Still, I stumbled, trying to explain, "The cook at the house I'm employed at."

"Oh, yeah? Where do you work at?" He swung a wrench in his hand rather menacingly.

"The Thornberry Manor." Even as the words slipped out of my mouth I had a stab of regret. Why on earth did I get so specific?

He nodded. "I know her, and this isn't her car."

Fantastic. I should have known that the people of Thornberry Manor were well known in a small town like this.

Mary jumped in. "We're taking care of her since she could seriously use an oil change. She doesn't exactly think of those types of things."

"Fine, drop it off and I'll get it done. But tell your friend she owes me." he said, his face relaxing as he gave her a wink.

"You got it." I said.

I left, with the impression that the reconnaissance had been unsuccessful and there was no way to rectify it.

Interesting, there was no other person in sight who seemed to own the blue car. I had counted on the oil change to break the ice with the mechanic.

"Alright, so how are you going to fake with Cook's car for this oil change? When are we doing that?" Mary asked.

"I messed that up." I groaned. "I panicked."

"Maybe we can tell her we want to treat her. Maybe she'll let us take it then."

"I guess I'll just come clean with her and hope she lets me take it."

"She probably will, I bet."

"Maybe we can drop it off in the morning."

"Let's go grab some of those doughnuts Cook really likes. And maybe a few salted caramels for Marguerite to sweeten the deal." Mary said, laughing.

I nodded my head in agreement. She smoothly merged onto the road.

We really needed to find another source besides Millie for information, especially since she seemed reluctant to share. Suddenly, I came up with another idea. I knew of another place where small town gossip was the main conversation.

"Tomorrow, when we do the oil change, you think you could you drop me by the salon? It's in a little brick building just before we get to the shopping mall."

"Oh, you're going to have a chat with the local hair stylist."
"That's what I always think of them as. Bartenders are the best at collecting information but are way tighter-lipped. But hairdressers? Maybe not."

I nodded with a grin. "Exactly."

"Just promise you are not going to let her whack all of that gorgeous hair off."

"I promise!" I said, and flicked my hair over my shoulder in a dramatic wave.

CHAPTER 9

The next morning started calm and relaxed, giving every appearance that today's escapade with Cook's car would go off without a hitch.

However, the calmness was soon destroyed, and before the breakfast dishes had even been cleared, Thornberry Manor was in the midst of a crisis.

First, poor Hank got his tail caught in the bedroom door as Lucy scooted to give Miss Janice her tray. The cat's screech frightened Lucy so much she dropped the tray, including Miss Janices's favorite teapot.

Fortunately, both Hank and the teapot were okay. He was quite offended, however, having been splashed by apple juice, along with my scream giving him a scare to add insult to injury. The cat streaked through the house, leaving drops of sticky juice all over the hardwoods.

It took us ages to clean the mess, nearly the entire morning. In the end, the air was thick with the scent of cleaning products, and we still had our regular chores to finish.

At long last, Mary and I stood before Cook, ready to present our carefully crafted plan.

We told her as concisely as we could. She raised her near nonexistent eyebrows and pushed her sparkling headband higher in her frizzy hair.

"My car? An oil change?" she asked. "What are you two crazy girls talking about?"

And so everything had to be explained again.

Finally, Cook, grumbling slightly, snatched her keys, the jingle echoing through the air. "Carl, huh? He's a scallawag. Like as not will make off with my muffler."

We laughed, nervously.

"Well, here you are. Let me get you some money."

"No! No," we exclaimed. "This is our treat."

I was happy I could do something for her. She always looked out for all of us.

"You two be back by two? I'm sure Marguerite will need you by then. And I can't cover for you again."

We promised we would, and scampered off through the back door. The hidden brick path led us through the herb garden. The air was filled with the sweet aroma of thyme, rosemary, and lavender. The vibrant colors of the flowers danced before our eyes, while the gentle rustling of the leaves seemed to cheer us on.

"You ready to do this?" Mary asked.

I nodded. "He's a very hard nut to crack."

"That's okay. That's my expertise—getting men to talk," she said with a wicked grin.

"Oh, I see, Miss Femme Fatale." I laughed.

She dramatically pursed her lips and fluttered her lashes. "He's in big trouble. Meet you there." With a fluff of her wild hair, she got in her car.

I got into Cook's car and tried to familiarize myself with the old sedan. With a rattle and a squeak of the brakes, I was right behind her.

A short time later, we pulled into the hidden driveway. I parked in front of the garage and met Mary who was already in the office.

Carl was there, looking just as scruffy and scrubby as last time. No, this time he actually looked worse. His skin had a strange pallor. He barely glanced in our direction and gave no indication of getting up.

"So you're back, " he said wryly and with a grimace. "You have the keys?" he asked, holding out a calloused hand that had grease embedded underneath every nail, turning them all into black half-moons.

I passed them over the counter, the metal clinking, and wondered how to start my conversation.

Mary turned toward him with a cigarette hanging out of the corner of her mouth. "You got a light?" she asked, casually taking it out and holding it between two slim fingers.

I almost choked. I'd never even seen her with a cigarette in my life.

Oddly, Carl's stare mirrored mine, only with an added frown of disgust. "I don't smoke. Those are bad for you."

I took a mental step back at his statement since it kind of derailed my ongoing theory.

"Did you ever smoke?" she asked.

"Never. The only vice I have is eating red meat."

"What about car racing?" she positively purred.

"Racing cars isn't a vice," he said, stoutly. "It's a gift."

"Oh, I see," she said smoothly and tucked the cigarette back into the crumpled pack. "I was wondering about race cars," she said.

I took a step back and let her take the reins. She was doing much better than I could.

"Yeah?" He seemed bored, or sick, or both.

"I've always been fascinated with car racing."

He grunted in response. I raised an eyebrow at her as if to say, "See, I told you he was difficult."

She didn't give up. "Do you race often?"

"Not enough," was his response. "Pay for the oil change now."

She pulled a card out of her wallet. "What car do you race?"

He ran it through an antique credit card machine and passed the card back. "That little Datsun outside the garage," he said. "You can ask anybody. They all know that car."

I narrowed my eyes. I bet they did.

"Now, hey," she said. "Weren't you part of the race with Brandon? I heard he raced you, and he won."

CEECEE JAMES

The look he gave her could have knocked a gargoyle off a church precipice. "I can't believe you'd believe that foolishness. It never happened," he said. "No one in this town can beat me. The idiot thought he could because he got his car suped up but guess who suped it up? Me. And he never paid me for the parts. But I'm going to be getting them back; don't you worry."

"How are you going to get them back?"

"I said, don't you worry. I have my ways," he growled. "Your car will be ready in a few hours. I got a new guy, so it may not take that long."

Mary nodded and waved goodbye. I followed her out to her car, not at all sure of what to make of Carl.

"Alrighty, Miss Detective, where to next?" Mary asked.

I frowned, trying to remember anything else that Brandon had said that last day.

"Oh! His work! Brandon said he overheard something about the cave from someone at his new job. Someone there has to know about it."

"Where did he work?" Mary asked.

"I'm not sure. He just got the job." I slumped into the seat.

"What did he say was in it?"

84

"Some kind of treasure."

"Treasure, huh? You know what that reminds me of?"

I looked at her, questioningly.

"Those gold mines over on Loften Road."

I arched my brow. "Gold mines? That seems like a beehive of motives."

I suddenly remembered Mary with the cigarette. "Wait. When did you start smoking?"

She laughed. "I didn't. But you told me about that cigarette butt you found. So I figured maybe our suspect is a smoker."

"Good thinking! I wouldn't have thought about using cigarettes as a way to suss out our suspect."

Mary gave me a wink. "I've got to be more useful than just my chauffeuring abilities."

"You are much more than that," I said.

"Now let's go check out these mines."

Finding the road and mines on the GPS and getting there wasn't an issue. The large guarded gate, cameras, and an unwavering guard was.

"Do you know if this was his new job?" Mary asked, staring

out through the windshield. "Because sneaking a bit of gold would be awful tempting to someone in serious debt."

"No," I said miserably.

From the small parking area outside of the gate, we could see a large multistory building. Off to the side was a road that led into a tunnel that large trucks came through.

"What did he say about the treasure?" Mary asked. "Try to remember."

"I'm not sure." I shook my head and tried to remember anything he would have mentioned. "I know he worked with a friend, a guy named Kyle."

She glanced at her watch. "We have an hour left before we need to get the car. Here goes nothing."

Mary exited the car. Shoulders thrown back, chin in the air, she walked over to the guard shack, her walk turning more into a sashay as she got closer.

A window on the front of the small building opened. Mary leaned forward, her head tilted to one side. One hand started twisting a lock of hair. I shook my head and tried not to laugh.

The two spoke for a minute. She shot him a smile and slowly made her way back.

"So I told them I was Laura Lee, Brandon's girlfriend...."

I gasped.

"Don't worry! They gave their condolences and are going to let his friend Kyle know my number so he can contact me about the funeral arrangements."

"Wow! Amazing job!" I gave her a big grin. "You should just go into acting."

"This is more fun. Maybe I should be an undercover cop or something." She said. "Let's go check on the car while we wait for that call."

We were on our way there when the phone call came.

"This Laura Lee?"

"Yes...."

"This is Kyle, Brandon's friend from the mine. I'm guessing you and I need to have a talk about some things."

I shot Mary a wide-eyed look. Finally we would get some answers.

CHAPTER 10

When we picked up Cook's car, Carl was no where in sight. There was no sign of the supposed new guy either. Just the keys left on the receipt.

Mary was aghast. "Anyone could have stolen it!" She said as she snatched it up.

I didn't think too many thieves would be beating down the door for a chance at Cook's car, but I still agreed.

We drove back home and entered yet another yummy scent day at the Manor. Marguerite making her homemade blackberry jam. Accepting her keys back, Cook nodded at Marguerite. "Making a mess in my kitchen."

"Making a treasure," Marguerite shot back.

Cook sniffed and said, "My recipe has been handed down through my family for over two hundred years. That's a treasure."

Marguerite retorted, "Two hundred years. That explains why it doesn't gel right. The secret is good fruit. I only buy fruit from Roseburgh. They have the ripest and juiciest blackberries, positively bursting with flavor and natural pectin."

I popped a plump berry into my mouth and agreed.

Cook shook a towel at her and turned back to her bread.

I watched Marguerite measure out the perfect amount of sugar, and wondered why so much jelly lately. More for the charity?

With an air of satisfaction, she gently poured the sugar into the pot. The blackberries simmered on the stove, and their aroma filled the kitchen.

"How long do you have to cook them?" I asked.

"Just long enough for them to release their natural juices and blend harmoniously with the sugar. Now,"

The next time I returned to the kitchen it seemed the blackberry mixture had transformed into a thick and luscious jam. She skillfully poured the jam into sterilized jars.

Cook tutted with a disapproving glance. "You have to wipe the rims, Marguerite. It's been too long since you've done this. Dust for brains."

"Dust for brains. Like what's on your lids because no one wants to use them," Marguerite barked back. Forehead wrinkled in concentration,, she ensured that each jar was filled to the brim. "And you should have your eyes checked. There's not a speck of jam on these rims." She set the seal and then placed the jars into the water bath.

Marguerite gave me permission for a hair cut during my lunch break the next day. Her kind expression made me think she still felt sorry for me, until she tacked on that she wanted me to look my best for the funeral, since I would be representing the Manor.

I swallowed and thanked her, and hurried off for the laundry.

***

The entire morning seemed off. As I bustled about, I kept hearing some whispers that stopped every time I came into the room.

"What's going on?" I asked Marguerite.

"Shh, it's nothing. Now, go bring this pile up to the laundry and give Jane a hand up there."

Curious, I did as I was asked.

Later, when Mary and I left at lunchtime she seemed as clueless as I was about the curious air in the manor.

She dropped me off outside the hairdressers, giving me a little wave before pulling back out to do a bit of shopping for Cook.

I raised my eyes to the imposing brick building, its sturdy structure casting a shadow on the bustling street. A twinge of unease crept over me, as I pondered my impulsiveness. Would the salon be swarming with customers and adamantly opposed to spontaneous walk-ins?

A glance up the road showed Mary was long gone, making any second guessing of this trip pointless. Squaring my shoulders, I pushed open the door and walked into the bright, hair-spray scented reception area.

The typical display of various hair products was set up on glass shelves. Curious, I glanced at the price of one and balked. Four times the amount of anything I ever paid.

Posters of models displaying formal and super chic hairstyles papered the walls. A long coffee table sat covered with stacks of fashion magazines in front of four chairs. Across from them was a high counter with a computer monitor and cash register, along with a telephone.

Which was ringing.

Someone slightly older than me responded to it. With her long nails, she delicately flicked away a spare wisp of her perfectly coiffed blonde hair. It had both highlights and lowlights. She gave me a bright red lipped smile and held up one finger.

I patiently stood by, the room filled with the soft hum of conversation and the faint scent of hair products. As she took the hair reservation, I couldn't help but notice a vibrant flash of green gum, glistening in her mouth.

A minute later, she turned her attention to me. "Hello, sugar, what can I do you for?" she asked.

Her warm smile made me grin back. "Hello, I was wondering if I could get a wash and a trim. I feel bad for not making an appointment."

"You are in luck! I don't have anyone else for a bit and I am bored out of my mind. Plus, I would love to sink my fingers into those lovely locks."

I followed her back to one of the chairs in front of the mirrored wall. The usual accumulation of jars with various combs and pins and brushes cluttered the counter.

"Why, aren't you the cutest little thing," the hairdresser said when she put me in the chair. "My name is Chelsea." She pumped the chair up and up and up and up and up. "I haven't had to do this much work since the last kid that was in here. Can you even drive yet?"

I snorted, surprised. I was short, but not that short. "Yes, of course I can."

She laughed gently and patted my shoulder. "Well, honey, with that smooth skin, I'm sure you get asked those questions all the time. One day, you'll appreciate it. Now, what are you wanting me to do for you today?" She ruffled my hair and smiled. "Your hair sure is a lovely color."

"Aw, thank you. Mostly, I just want the ends trimmed," I said.

"No problem." She took me over to get my hair washed first, which I thoroughly enjoyed. It had been a while since my last haircut. I closed my eyes and let the massage nearly put me to sleep, if only it weren't for the hard plastic curve of the sink under my neck.

Then she brought me back in the chair and adjusted the plastic cape around my shoulders. With practiced efficiency, she sprayed my hair down with leave-in conditioner. "So, I don't believe I have seen you around here before. Are you new to town?"

I loved how small the town was that they could see a newcomer come in and notice them easily. However, that also made it difficult for me to ask questions because usually that meant they were also suspicious about any newcomers.

"No, I work at the Thornberry Manor. Do you know of it?" I asked, squinting at the mirror. What was it about the mirrors in salons that made one look especially homely?

"Oh, sure! I love that place! And how are things going there? Is it as glamorous as I think it is? I've seen a few shots of charity events she's had there."

"It's an amazing place." I smiled, knowing I spoke the truth.

"Do you work with a bunch of friends? Do you ever get out into town?"

"I think we're all good friends there. And I do get out in town." I bit my lip, realizing how hard it was going to be to actually talk about this.

She paused what she was doing and shot me a sympathetic glance. "Aw, honey. You just tell me what's the matter. I'm a wonderful listener."

"One of my friends was Brandon. He—" I stopped.

Her eyebrows lifted up. "Poor Brandon," she said, shaking her head. Her comb went back to flicking layers. "I always told that boy he was on the fast track for destruction."

"So you knew him? Were you guys close?"

"I sure did. We grew up together, and from kindergarten. He's always been in trouble. Were you friends?" She gave me a knowing look. "Or...was it growing into something a bit more?"

"Becoming more. At least I'm pretty sure we were," I said. "We actually explored that cave right before he died, it was like our first real date."

"Oh, you poor thing!" Her face drew tight as she frowned. Her scissors snipped. "You know, that cave was something of a surprise. I've lived here all these years and never even knew it was there. Still something bad was bound to happen with the toes he was stepping on...Especially because he lost out on that dumb bet."

"I heard about this, I think."

"Well, I don't like talking ill of the dead and all, especially seeing he meant something to you. I don't want to taint that image."

"It's okay. Don't worry. I like talking about him, to be honest."

"Well, he had a bet going with the owner of that mechanic shop. He lost it, and lost it bad, but he never paid." At this, she raised one eyebrow to indicate what kind of person she thought of a character who did not pay their bets. "Not the best impression. Isn't my place to say, but that relationship was probably not headed on the best path. Brandon didn't mean to be trouble, but he definitely was. Didn't seem to be able to help himself."

I knew Carl had done it. Killed him since Brandon hadn't paid him. I struggled to control my fury. "That's terrible."

"Sure is," she said combing my hair again. She snipped off a little bit. "How's that look? Good length?"

"Perfect," I said as she continued to check the length.

She took a tiny snip. "So from what I've heard through Carl, he still is planning to collect on his bet."

"Who could he collect from now?"

"I think he's trying to get Brandon's old car, since it'll be worth about the same. He swears he can get all of his parts back out of it that he put in it. See, he helped Brandon get it going good and fast for the races but if Brandon lost, he had to pay up for all the work."

That proved even more of a motive. And, that explained why Brandon had been so nervous about his car being left on the side of the road.

I changed the subject. "So you really had heard nothing about that cave, huh?"

"No, never. Not even my grandfather, who's lived his whole life here, knew about that cave."

"Would you believe that when we were there, I swear somebody else was there, too." I explained about the sound of a gunshot and how scared Brandon had seemed when he hurried me back to the car.

Her eyes lit up. "Shut up! No way."

"I'm serious. So you wouldn't know anybody that would have maybe been out there too?"

My phone gave a notification from Mary that she was all done and checking out at the store.

"Sorry, sis," she said before combing my hair back. She turned me around. "This town is small. I feel like I would've heard if anybody ever discovered that cave before, and especially if there were any dangerous things about it. Now do you want a blow-out?" She brushed off a few stray hairs.

I shook my head. My intention was to save up money specifically to give her a substantial tip as a token of gratitude for her immense help. I followed through, and she grinned at the final amount.

"You come back now, anytime," she said.

I assured her I would and headed for the door. I could see Mary pulling into the parking lot.

Chelsea called me just as I reached it. "Hey, I just thought of something. We also have karaoke night on Fridays. You should come join us sometime. It's a hoot. We do it at the hotel in town."

"Okay, that sounds good," I said.

"All right hon, you take care of yourself!"

I gave a wave and smile and ran out to Mary's awaiting car.

"What do you think?" I asked, shaking my hair around my shoulders.

"Not too short, so I would say it's a success on the hairdo front. Now what about gossip? Any winning tidbits there?"

I filled Mary in on what the hairdresser had told me.

"Sounds like Marguerite might have been on the money with her opinions about Brandon." She saw my face and grimaced. "I'm sorry, Laura Lee. I shouldn't have said that. It isn't fair and doesn't matter."

"It might matter, if its what got him killed."

Maybe I had been looking at Brandon with rose-colored glasses. But that didn't mean I could change the fact that I had really cared about him and my heart was still broken about what we could have had. Maybe I would have been what changed his life.

Instead, I had just come along too late.

CHAPTER 11

That night, after final chores, we both dressed conservatively with light jackets. The temperature dropped once the sun went down, despite the hot days.

Mary drove to the small park that Kyle had told us about.

"Ready for this?"

"So ready."

We walked over to the picnic area. Darkness had descended and the soft glow of the lampposts guided our way. The sound of crickets filled the air, their rhythmic chirping creating a sweet melody. We sat on the weathered wooden bench as the cool evening breeze filtered through the tree leaves. We settled in, ready to meet the person who held the potential to unravel the mystery and clear everything up.

A pair of squirrels chased each other up and down the big oak trees. I wondered when they'd go to sleep, and where that was. My imagination took me to a cozy little hollow from a picture book I'd had when I was a child.

"The funeral is coming up soon. How are you holding up?" Mary asked. She had angled toward me, her eyes soft with concern, and now watched my face carefully. "In all this business, I feel like I haven't asked it enough."

"I'm coping, I guess." If I said it enough, it would come true, right? Really, I just wanted to spend the afternoon locked in the little secret garden, under a tree in the moss with Hank to keep me company.

"You want me to come? Because I will."

"It's up to you. It would be nice to have the support, but I'll be okay."

Her eyes narrowed slightly. "Can I say that it seems you're using this investigation thing as a way to stay busy and not think about your emotions. It might catch up with you out of the blue."

I nodded. "I'll be okay."

She nudged my shoulder with a sisterly pat. "Emotions aren't terrible, you know."

That got a smile out of me. "Only slightly."

She stiffened. "I think our guy is here." She gave a discreet nod toward the parking area.

I turned to look.

A small man, with shoulders as wide as his height, approached us at a slow pace. He wore a faded black t-shirt and tight jeans. He glanced in our direction, then raised black eyebrows and gave us a wave.

"Is it bad he reminds me of a thumbtack?" Mary whispered under her breath.

I nearly choked with laughter. Before I could completely recover he called out, "I'm Kyle. Which of you is Laura Lee?"

I raised my hand and attempted to clear my mind of any thoughts related to thumbtacks. "That's me. This here is my friend, Mary."

He grinned. "Nice to meet you." With athletic ease, he sat in the bench opposite of us. "Brandon mentioned you a few times. I'm not sure how serious you guys were getting, but I know he was pretty serious about you."

I didn't realize how much I needed to hear those words. My heart squeezed with a mixture of warmth and pain.

Then a sadness hit that he never got to tell me how he felt himself.

I tried my best to control the emotions. "We were taking it slow. He seemed to have a lot going on he didn't want to talk about."

Kyle laughed then, and it sounded nasty. "Yeah, he was in a bit of a pickle about that car."

Mary arched an eyebrow. She seemed to home in on his tone, being a sarcastic queen herself.

I had to respond quickly. Who knew what she would say? "So I heard. Something about him having the car worked on by Carl. Then he bet it all and lost the race and still owed Carl for the parts."

"It was a mess. I get it. He loved racing and loved that car and it needed work. But laying it all on the line and not having a plan in case he lost—that wasn't his best idea." Kyle shook his head. "Guess it doesn't matter now."

"Carl thinks he's still going to get paid somehow," Mary blurted. "We were just at his shop. He had a lot to say about it."

"Course he did. He filed a civil dispute when Brandon hemmed and hawed about payment. Court ruled that Brandon either had to pay or return the parts. Probably will get settled in probate."

Not even a week had passed since the poor man's death, and Carl was already scheming to profit from it.

He had to be the one who cut the rope.

"Did Brandon have a side job planned?" I pressed. "Something that might help him pay the money back?"

Nervously, Kyle fidgeted on the bench. His jaw clenched a few times.

That was an interesting response. "He did, didn't he?" I pressed. "Was it something bad?"

He had better answer me, because I had to know.

"Maybe. It could just be him blowing smoke. He was known for that. After all, he said he had some powerful friends."

Was that a lie? I had chills. "What did he say?"

"He mentioned something about doing some maintenance and groundskeeping for some rich guy." Kyle rubbed his head. "But...I don't know. I felt like there was something he wasn't saying about it."

"What do you mean?" I could feel my heart racing. What was true, and what wasn't? I felt a bit scared to find out about some nefarious side of Brandon I hadn't seen coming.

Kyle exhaled deeply. I stole a glance at Mary, silently urging the guy to divulge whatever he was hanging onto. Perhaps my pushing too hard would result in nothing.

"He owed a lot to Carl. Like...he would need to do a lot of jobs to even make a dent. So, how could just one job do it for him? Yet, he was convinced this one guy's house was all he needed to do."

"Did he say what the rich guy's name was?" Mary asked.

Kyle shook his head. "Not one word about who it was or where."

This conversation was just creating more questions. I tried thinking of something Kyle could answer.

"What about the cave?" I asked.

Kyle looked confused.

I continued, "Brandon mentioned hearing about a possible treasure in the cave where he passed away. He took me to it the day before but we thought we heard someone and then what sounded like a gunshot."

Kyle's eyes widened as he exclaimed, "I had no idea? Are the police aware of that?"

"I told them but they shrugged it off."

"That doesn't surprise me. We work in a gold mine. There is always conspiracies and theories and rumors of hidden stashes and stuff. I don't know why Brandon would suddenly believe one of them and take off with it."

"But you don't know or remember anything about that specific cave? And anything about his powerful friends?"

He smirked, making my nerves ratchet up. "Not that I can recall."

Mary checked her watch and then looked up at me. We were running out of time. I wasn't sure how much more we could get from Kyle. Other than his suspicions and the slim chance he was involved, he really seemed confused as well. His face reflected the same hurt and grief I had.

Honestly, I had a sinking feeling about my suspect list. I didn't think Kyle was involved after all.

Out of nowhere, Mary revealed a pack of cigarettes. When she offered one to Kyle, he shook his head.

"No, thanks," he said. " I quit about a year ago. I got enough lung problems from the mines."

"Oh," she smiled sweetly in the way guys never could resist. A smile I could never make. I'll admit I quit trying when the man asked me if I had a stomach cramp. "Do you have a lighter, by chance?"

"Nope. Sorry. I never really was good at keeping up with them. Went through disposables enough to almost need a new one every time I bought a pack."

"Eh, I can wait a bit longer. Trying to kick it myself." Mary said, slipping the pack off the table. I gave her a smile.

That pretty much finished most of my evidence. But I did have one more question.

"I apologize if I'm coming across as too interrogative. I have this strong feeling that something is lacking."

His posture didn't relax, especially, when I added, "I just wondered about one more thing."

"And that is...?"

"Are you sure I'm not offending you?"

"Nah, I completely understand. He was my friend and I think something is off, too. If you can figure it out, I'm at your disposal. Whatever I can do to help."

"Do you know anything about a pocketknife he had? Wooden

handle with some sort of phoenix or something engraved on it?"

"Oh, yeah." He reached into his pocket and pulled out a very similar knife. This one had his name carved into it with a little dragon. Yet, I noticed the identical small stylized flame being held up by the creature, just like the one on Brandon's knife. "A few years ago, some of us got hold of these. After an incident in the mines, we persevered and came out stronger. It was kind of a miracle that no one was seriously hurt and no lives lost. It ended up being our way of celebrating making it through, you know? The bond between survivors."

He seemed like he'd softened. I nodded. "Brandon dropped his. It was at the scene at the cave."

"The scene....Oh," Kyle said. He slid the knife back into his pocket. A few seconds of quiet built between us. I felt my stomach drop as I realized the knife wasn't a clue after all.

"Well, thank you, Kyle." I said, standing up. "I appreciate you calling, meeting, and dealing with the third degree."

He smiled sadly at me. "It helps, I guess. It hurts to see how this affects you, but I admire your determination to uncover the truth. It really sucks that he couldn't spend more time with you and have the future you guys could have. I am happy to learn that you embody everything he believed, and even more.

I felt something in me hitch. I gulped and sweated and my eyes burned. No one tells you how grief comes out of every pore in your body. I could barely breathe.

Mary thanked Kyle. I took a few deep breaths and faked my way through our parting. We all shook hands and parted ways.

In the car, Mary said nothing. I stared out the window and felt the tears finally let go of my lashes.

CHAPTER 12

*H*ank pushed through the crack in the wainscoting and gracefully navigated around the bookshelf. I rolled to watch him pad soundlessly across the wood floor.

"Good morning," I whispered. Hank meowed back contentedly and his green eyes squinted shut in a little kitten smile.

I could only give him a little pet, though, because chores were calling. I felt guilty for neglecting my duties the past few days with all my focus and running around with questions about Brandon. So, as quick as I could, I got ready and ran down to the kitchen.

Cook jumped when I rushed in. "Heaven's girl, you surprised me."

I grabbed an apron and made my way over to the sink to wash dishes. They had piled up, to match the amazing food she'd prepared. Yeasty scents of fresh bread and cinnamon rolls mingled with the brown roasted scent of meat. My stomach rumbled.

"Is Miss Janice having guests tonight?" I asked, deducing it from the huge serving dish waiting on the counter.

"Yes, she is, and I'm tired." Cook sat in a chair with her feet propped on the spare next to her. She brushed back a sweaty curl that had escaped her headband. "She sprang it on me at dinner last night. I had Lucy nip down to the butchers, and as luck would have it, they had a rack of lamb."

"I'm sorry I wasn't here to help."

She smiled kindly. "Now don't you worry about it. You just keep getting better from your young friend. Have you heard anything new?"

"Not really. No. But both Mary and I are convinced that he didn't accidentally die out at that cave."

Just saying those words out loud made me feel kind of sick again. I turned back to the soapy sink. Mary came in then.

"Ah, there you are my petunia," Cook beamed. Then she scowled. "Did you just track in wet leaves on my nice clean floor?"

"Hi, Cook." She smiled as she tied on her apron. Her eyes caught mine. "Did you tell her what we learned?"

"She was just starting to do that before you tromped in. And before you begin, you mind getting me a bit of hot water for my tea?"

With a tip of the kettle, Mary filled a teacup with steaming hot water. She handled it delicately as she brought it over. I quickly filled Cook in as I washed a stack of plates.

Cook reached for a chamomile teabag from the basket always kept on the table. "I know one thing. If he had a racing debt it had to be several thousand dollars." Cook mused. "And to try to earn it from one job? It must have been a big house with big trees or a big yard or something. You are definitely looking for a rich guy."

"You have any ideas on how we start looking for this rich guy? We keep coming up to dead ends."

I added, "And nothing is leading back to that cave."

"How did you ever hear about that cave anyway?" Cook asked, dipping her tea bag in the water.

I continued working through the dishes. "Brandon told me he heard something about it the other day."

"Well, who did he hear it from?"

I shook my head. "He just said he overheard it at work." A big pile of bubbles spilled over the side and slid down the counter. Before Cook could see, I wiped them with a rag.

"While Kyle doesn't remember being told about it, he did mention the ongoing rumors concerning the gold they handle."

"Maybe you should try to put together Brandon's last day," Cook said. "Figure out where he was, where he could have gone, and what he was doing."

"I wouldn't know where to start, really." I replied, feeling a bit helpless.

"We should go to Brandon's house, next" Mary said, taking charge. "I can't believe we completely skipped that step."

"Tomorrow?"

"Investigating seems to be our new lunch time tradition."

Hank came in then and rubbed against my ankles. His little collar with its special charm glistened in the overhead light. It reminded me of the lighter.

"One lie down, Hank. How many more to go?"

· · ·

* * *

Once again, we left at our lunch time, with a few granola bars and some bottles of water, and headed out to Brandon's house.

The sun shone brightly overhead, casting a warm happy glow on the green fields we passed by. It created a cheerful mood that was totally the opposite of how I felt.

"Do you think the door will be locked?" Mary asked, breaking the silence.

"Maybe," I said. "But I know where the key is."

She gave me a sympathetic glance and concentrated on the drive.

Memories from the last time I'd been down this road filled my head. He had invited me over to play some game with little pegs. Cribbage, I think. I'd never been a game person but I did my best, and he'd been a pretty patient teacher. Afterward we'd gone outside where he lit a bonfire and listened to the crickets and the frogs. As the sun set through the trees, I thought he might kiss me.

And yet we had parted as friends, and I had gone home with a feeling of missing something.

We turned the corner and there it was. White siding with a green front door, and an over-grown lawn. I swallowed hard.

Although the house looked similar to the last time I saw it, it had a completely different vibe. It was as if it recognized its emptiness and the absence of its owner.

"Kind of out of the way back here," Mary said, staring at the trees that crowded the tiny, rough road.

"Yeah, it is. All these little houses are tucked in here and there."

She pulled into the driveway, and we climbed out. The neighbor's dogs immediately started barking. The shaggy lawn made me a bit sad to see.

"Come on," I said, beckoning to her as I walked up to the front door. He kept his spare key underneath an old planter, one whose plant had died long ago. I tipped the plastic bucket up and saw it there with relief. Quickly, I unlocked the door, and we walked inside.

The state of the house was untidy and covered in dust. It didn't seem like it had been ransacked or vandalized. Brandon had obviously been somewhat messy.

It made me upset to see his breakfast dishes still in the sink where he thought he'd be back to wash them, and hamburger defrosting in the fridge. Hadn't anyone in his family come to clean up? Sadly, I walked over to the table while Mary slowly went into the living room.

It was there that I spotted a paper plate with writing all over it.

"I found something!" I shouted. He had written a to-do list for the job Kyle had mentioned. "He really was going to go take care of somebody's yard maintenance."

"How can you tell?" Mary tried to look.

"See here? He has a tool written down." I googled it real quick to find out what it was. It turned out to be a saw specifically for pruning tall trees.

"Do you think this would pay in the thousands?" I asked Mary. It seemed bananas to me.

She raised an eyebrow. "He put dollar signs all around it, and a big arrow, so it must have been."

"How on earth are we going to find it? Our only clue is tall trees." I felt drained with all these small hints that didn't seem to lead us anywhere.

Mary tapped the envelope. "This is kind of interesting. Notice how he wrote 'red door' with the dollar signs, too? You think it's the same place? Or was it that he had multiple jobs?"

"I'm not sure." I said. "Right about now it feels as difficult as finding a needle in a haystack."

"Pish-posh! Tall trees, red door," she repeated adamantly. "And it has to be in town because Brandon said he never took any long trips, right?"

"Yeah, I suppose that's right." I admitted.

"So how do we find rich people who have tall trees?"

"How's that?"

"Look for a red door." Mary confidently declared, her voice filled with determination.

CHAPTER 13

Saturday came. The house was in chaos preparing for Miss Janice's charity event. And it was even more chaotic because Marguerite, Mary, and I would not be there.

I stood in front of the bathroom mirror and studied myself. I could only see to my waist, but it didn't matter. I wore a simplistic knee-length black dress. My hair was twisted into a loose braid, and I barely touched any makeup. I didn't want to cry but I feared it was a possibility and didn't want to risk the mess.

"Ready?" Mary asked. She had on one of her flowy dresses, but a rare black one without her usual blast of color. Marguerite had thought it would be nice for her to be there as support.

Marguerite wore a dark navy pantsuit. When she first came around the corner, it took everything I had to squelch my surprise and not make a big deal out it. I'd never seen her in pants before.

We all piled into Mary's little car with Cook's reassurances that the manor would still be standing when we returned ringing in our ears. Marguerite sat up front, while I sat in the center of the backseat. I had so many thoughts rustling through my mind, it felt as if silence would be deafening.

But Mary started chattering right away, not leaving me to stew. "Marguerite, do you know of someplace around here where rich people live who have tall trees and maybe one of the houses has a red door?"

"Not really." She squinted, thoughtfully. "The house has a red door, specifically?"

Mary explained the clue we had found at Brandon's house.

Marguerite lips pursed. "This does remind me of something. However, for me, the Red Door is a place. It's an antique shop. Perhaps he was looking for an old treasure?"

"An antique shop?" I asked.

"Yes. It's a rather darling little place. With all the old families and mines and history in this area, it has quite a few unique things. In fact, some of those antique pieces in the study came from there. Mr. Thornsberry used to adore antique shopping and often brought home bits of this and that. Of course, the style nearly put Miss Janice's nose out of joint. So he kept it hidden in his study."

"Oh! Like that spindle with the wheel?" Mary asked, her eyes alight like an excited kid.

"Yes. That would be one such item." She paused for a moment, and then glanced back at me. "Would you care to go afterward, Laura Lee?"

I nodded, quite surprised at her asking. Bring Marguerite on a sleuthing excursion? The idea fascinated me.

"What about Miss Janice's party?"

"Cook did say she could handle it," Marguerite said with a sly smile. "Maybe this will be good for her to see what I really do."

"Thank you, Marguerite." I gave her a smile, albeit a weak one.

We arrived at the church early. I was surprised by the abundance of cars already there.

Marguerite led our little group through the front door. The scent of freshly cut flowers mingled with the faint aroma of burning candles, created a bittersweet fragrance.

We entered the sanctuary, where I immediately froze with grief. Resting on a pedestal at the front was a glossy wooden box. The casket's top was adorned with an array of spilled flowers, with a small photo of him positioned on a stand nearby.

I sucked in a breath as tears blurred my eyes. Marguerite patted my arm and then handed me her hanky. Seeing the little fabric square, all carefully trimmed in lace, made me smile a bit.

"Thank you," I whispered.

"You keep it, love. I brought another." She patted me again.

The muted lighting cast a melancholic glow, highlighting the floral arrangements adorning the casket. Hushed whispers filled the air, mingling with occasional sniffles and quiet sobs. As I gathered my thoughts, a heavy feeling weighed upon my heart, a mix of sorrow and gratitude for the memories shared.

Things were slow to start and we occasionally got odd glances from people who didn't recognize me. Irene came in and made a beeline as soon as she saw me.

"Laura Lee, my dear, how are you doing?" she asked.

"I'm okay. Taking things day by day." I replied.

"Marguerite, how have you been?"

"I'm doing okay, Irene. I am so sorry to hear about Brandon, I really am."

The service started and she made sure to sit next to me.

"Any luck on poking around?" Irene whispered.

"We're working on it. We have a few leads involving his racing habits and possibly a gardening job he did."

She gave me a look of surprise. "That is an odd combination. I have to say, I regret not knowing more about his life and what he had going on." She shook her head. "Silly boy. Oh, how I do miss his smile."

"Me too," I said, and instantly felt the first tingle of tears.

As I heard Brandon's family reminisce about his younger years, it became clear that they had little to share about his life as a grown-up. That made me even more upset. Why had they cut him out? Racing seemed to be his biggest vice. Many people had much worse ones.

Eventually the time came for his brothers and uncles to come lift the casket.

We bowed our heads and waited as the pastor stepped forward and began reading.

I could hear the subtle sniffles from Irene. I put my arm around her waist and leaned my head against her shoulder.

The prayers seemed to take forever and yet were over in a flash. The wooden box held the man I had been falling in love with.

The pastor read a scripture of how Jesus wept when his friend had died. It struck me that he understood grief. He had been sad, broken-hearted even, although he knew he would be raising Lazarus from the dead.

My mind spun around that for a bit while the pastor talked. We stood for a song, and then it was done.

Slowly, people began to disperse.

As our little group walked away, Irene straightened herself. I wiped my eyes with the tissue that Mary had pressed into my hand.

"I have complete confidence in your ability to uncover the truth about him. While Brandon may have been foolish about certain things, his death was not due to an accident. If you need me, call."

When we got to the car, Irene gave me her number. She brought me in for a big squeeze. "I can see so much why he liked you. You got fire in you, girl."

Marguerite sighed. "She's right. And the more I hear, I am beginning to think there is something very fishy going on."

It was a relief to hear her say so. She was so down to earth, if she believed it, it had to be true.

I rifled through my purse until I found a small mirror. I stared at my eyes- red and puffy. My father would have said they looked like two pee-holes in the snow.

I snorted at the thought.

Marguerite eyed me as she struggled with the seatbelt.

"Sorry. Just a weird thought," I said as an excuse.

"No worries," she replied primly. "Now I say we go get some sustenance. Take us to Shelbies, please, Mary."

I raised an eyebrow at her bringing up the coffee shop. Marguerite despised coffee.

"They have tea as well," she spouted, catching my look. "Actually, we should have stopped by first. No disrespect to the dead but funerals are so difficult to sit through. Long, drawn out farewells in a crowd of people you either don't know or don't want to know. I prefer mourning in private."

"I understand that," I answered. "I am glad I got to say goodbye, but I also wish I didn't feel like so much of an unwanted spectacle."

Marguerite gave a loud snort.

"What? Goodness, Marguerite!" Mary said.

"I think most of those folks probably hadn't said a word, or at least a nice one, to Brandon in years. No one had one thing to say about his life right before he died. I'm pretty sure you and his aunt are probably the only two he would have thought belonged there the most."

"I noticed that, too. Everyone talked about him like he passed when he was sixteen or something," Mary said. "I'm sure he would have felt honored that you especially were there."

As sad as the subject was, the thought gave me even more of a sense of relief.

And I felt even better as we exited the car and walked up to the antique shop, with a functioning water wheel on one side, and one, very bright red door.

Rusty farm equipment long past use sat in the front yard. Horseshoes hung inverted above the door, a superstition about luck. We entered through the red door, with Mary staring it with big eyes.

Inside was a massive room full of shelves, cabinets, and furniture. It was so crowded I felt like my eyes were playing ping-pong around the building.

Near the door stood a tiny counter with an old woman sitting behind it. She seemed to be working on some knitting, while an old man was shuffling around not too far away. He carried a metal basket of glass milk bottles to some unknown opening amongst the many trinkets.

"Wow," I whispered.

"I told you. Very impressive." Marguerite said, before briskly walking to the lady at the register. "Betty, how are you?"

"So this must be the place. What are we looking for?" Mary asked.

I shrugged. "I don't know. I guess we just look around for a bit?" I asked, unsure of where to begin.

Mary and I separated to wander the shop. I couldn't help but pick up half the things I saw. Beautiful carnival glass bowls, sterling silver serving ware, old books with threadbare covers, and all the beautiful old furniture pieces with iron hinges and solid wood structures dinged and rubbed smooth from decades of use.

I was beginning to make my way back to the front when I saw an old mining lantern. On the base was a very familiar flame insignia, one I recognized from Brandon and Kyle's knives. The price was ten. That was a steal anyways, and so I carried it to the front with me.

"Ah, that one is a real local treasure," the lady, Betty, said as I sat it down.

"What does the little flame on it mean?" I asked.

"It's the old symbol for the gold mine outside of town, you know the one that had that big robbery recently?"

I know my mouth dropped open.

"I...hadn't heard about that." I said as Mary walked up.

"Yeah, they said that someone was taking the dust from the gold out in small batches, somehow. Hard to believe this would even be a new crime, but apparently it's true. The news says they think the total haul was somewhere in the range of ten million dollars."

"Oh, my," Marguerite said.

"My boyfriend worked there. His name was Brandon." I said and instantly saw a look of sadness, but no other emotion of surprise or caution.

"I heard about that poor boy. Funeral today?"

I nodded.

"I am so sorry, dear. I had no clue he worked at the mine. I'm sorry for your loss."

"Thank you. Did he ever come in here?" I asked.

"Hmm, maybe. I can't be sure. My memory isn't what it was." She turned and yelled, "James, did that Brandon boy ever come through here?"

The old man shuffled up to the counter.

"I believe so. He was asking about collectors and appraisers but didn't want to say what he wanted appraised so I couldn't help him much. I told him to try the internet." The man replied.

"Ah, well, thank you anyway." I said and paid for the lantern.

Betty wished us the best before we left to go back home. Once more I was collecting more questions than answers and things were starting to get very complicated.

CHAPTER 14

The manor *was* still standing, per Cook's promise. It was also filled with chaotic activity. Silverware clattered and voices chattered, filling the air. The aroma of freshly baked pastries wafted through the halls, mingling with the scent of polished wood. Excitement and anticipation hung in the air, making me quite curious.

Marguerite muttered as she took off her coat.

"What's going on?" Mary asked Lucy as she buzzed by with an armload of table linens.

"Just one sec," she said and rushed on, her shoes clattering against the hardwood.

Jane showed up with a vase filled with flowers. "It's been a minor emergency here. Check out the back room!"

"They dropped them off here?" Marguerite asked, surprised. "And Cook didn't turn them away?"

"Yes, and can you believe it? Skads of them! We hardly know what to do with it all!"

The doorbell rang. Jane paled. "More?" she whispered.

Butler answered it. "We aren't accepting any more donations."

"Where should we bring them then? Our children have been collecting them all week," an earnest woman answered.

I glanced around the corner to see the Sunday School teacher. She held two hefty-sized trash bags, with another at her feet.

Butler swallowed, and his jaw clenched. "Right this way, ma'am."

She wasn't able to carry them all. With a look of distaste, Butler carried one. He led her to the drawing room, and I followed.

My jaw dropped at the sight. Jessie and Lucy were rifling through the clothes, their movements filling the air with a sense of urgency. The sound of rustling fabrics and their strained whispers intermingled with the occasional clatter of hangers.

I turned and ran upstairs. On the way, patting the large knight statue on my way, to change out of my clothes.

Marguerite must have performed some sort of changing magic act, because she was already heading back down the stairs dressed in her normal work uniform.

I was right behind her. Not only did we have to get Miss Janice and her guests a late tea, we had to find a home for all the clothing.

For the next few hours, we worked like hungry chickens after crickets. I was exhausted by the time evening came around. The great hall grandfather clock chimed nine o'clock when Marguerite admitted defeat and sent us all to bed.

But bed was not for me, not after what I'd learned today at the antique store. Mary met me at the door to my room, obviously feeling the same way. We both jumped online to look up the news stories about the robbery at the gold mine.

We'd hardly started when there was a knock on the door.

Janet poked her head in. "Hungry?" she asked in a sing-song voice.

"Yes!" Mary yelled.

She held out a tray. It was basically a charcuterie board but with chunks of fluffy, fresh baked bread, large crumbles of sharp cheddar, and cubes of ham.

It took me about two seconds to realize I was very hungry. I hadn't eaten much today, what with the funeral, only to return to the three-ring-circus at the manor. Janet even had some homemade cookies.

Mary was in the middle of explaining what we were doing when Hank cracked open the cupboard door and stalked out. With a little butt wiggle, the orange cat leaped up onto a cozy bed.

Mary made a place for him but he ignored it. He had a special talent at not responding to overtures of affection if he wasn't feeling it.

I ignored him to give him space. Popping a piece of cheese in my mouth, I continued my search.

I was pretty impressed at what I'd found. Betty's estimate of hitting the ten million dollar mark was spot on. During the monthly dust weight audit, it was noticed that a particular amount was missing, indicating a theft. It seems that they had been underreporting weights for a while, but last month was significantly higher than usual. That's when they hypothesized that the person responsible for secretly taking and smuggling small amounts had successfully executed a final, larger operation.

"Wow! I'm amazed that they let it go on for so long without

realizing there was an issue, considering the high level of security and attention to detail," Mary pointed out.

"I agree. My guess is that someone involved in reporting was likely involved in this. Someone higher up." I said and then paused. "There's probably someone who makes a decent amount of money in a top position at a gold mine."

Mary nodded adamantly, her curls bobbing.

I frowned. "Wait, here is an article that says there was a truck involved. The dollar amount was unusually high because the previous major haul was stolen. An armored truck, designed to resemble a mint vehicle, took the gold but unfortunately experienced a breakdown not too far from the mines. The truck was located, but there is no trace or evidence left on it."

Mary's eyebrows lifted, and she nodded sagely. "So, someone may have stolen the actual mint truck, which they wouldn't have wanted anyone to know because it would make the security look weak."

"Yep. The gold mines had various government and contractor agreements, involving the owners, operators, and the mint, with a wealth of information available. It wouldn't take much to upset that balance and get some serious investigations rolling around the mine."

"But how would we even begin to figure out who would be

involved, whether they stored anything at the cave, and where they lived?"

"I'm not sure. Maybe it's time to talk to your dispatch friend again." I suggested.

"That's not a bad idea. I can tell her what we have found so far and see if she has anything new to tell us." She said, picking up her phone. "Here's what I texted.—**Hey, I was wondering if you wanted to do an info exchange. I can bring donuts!**"

"Now we wait." I said and sighed, leaning back on the pillows which gave Hank an excuse to explore the meat platter.

Janet shooed him away. He blinked annoyed eyes at her.

"I wish we could get some answers soon," Mary said.

"Me too."

She reached over and patted her lap to get Hank to join her. This time he did. "You goofy animal," she said and gave his head scratch.

Her phone dinged. —**I would love some donuts! Tomorrow morning, perhaps?**

She responded—Sure thing. I can swing by your work around eight.

Hank nudged my hand. I reached out to untangle his charm on his collar that had twisted backward. What an elegant little piece, an antique that Mr. Thornberry had bestowed on him.

He blinked his green eyes at me in appreciation. Then, with agile grace, he reached out a paw and snagged a cookie.

"Hank!" we all shouted.

With a mischievous glint in his eyes, he stealthily cleaned the crumbs tickling his whiskers.

"Time for bed, I guess," Janet said, cleaning up. "Tomorrow looks like it's also going to be a busy day."

CHAPTER 15

The next morning, the sweet chirping of birds woke us up. Just kidding. It was Marguerite who barked out orders while still trying to organize the clothing. Things got even more interesting when the doorbell rang with three more huge deliveries before the breakfast dishes had been cleared.

The deliveries worked in our favor though, because Marguerite finally gave up. She made the decision for us to the load the clothing and take it to the dry cleaners.

"All of them," she demanded, completely fed up.

So Lucy, Mary and I packed the bags in Cook's sedan. They piled across the back seat and we could barely shut the trunk.

On the way there, Mary noticed a pesky check engine light glowing on the car's dashboard. "Great. Somethings wrong."

"What if they didn't secure the oil pan drainage nut? It can cause the engine to seize up. That happened to my aunt, you know," Lucy offered helpfully.

While we unloaded the bags, Mary reached out to Carl. Although gruff, he told her to bring the car back in.

"After the next load of clothing, I'm going to swing by. You girls want to come with me?" Mary asked.

"Of course," we both said.

We practically had the place shut down as they cleaned and pressed all the clothes. Reputations were on the line, and Miss Janice, along with the manor, couldn't be associated with anything less than perfect.

The way back was slightly scary. The faint hum of the engine seemed slightly off, a disconcerting sound that lingered in the air. All I could think about was that oil pan.

Cook shook her head when we gave her the news. "I told you not to trust him."

"Well, you know, we wanted to talk with him."

"Seems like he didn't like how the talk went. You tell Carl if he let some boy try to pull some mechanic scam, we're going to have words."

Mary grinned. "You got it, Cook."

We dropped off another carload at the cleaners, who appeared decidedly less pleased to see us the second time, and then drove on to Highlands.

Mary pulled the car in front of the garage. We all marched inside.

"So just the light? No noises or issues or anything?" Carl asked, moving gingerly as he came around the desk.

"Are you okay?" I asked, feeling a wave of concern because he looked like he was in pain. Cook's words dissipated as I watched him wince.

"Just healing from appendicitis."

That was a surprise. "When did that happen?"

"A few days ago. It's why I hired that one guy but he turned out to be about useless, and I'm pretty sure he stole some parts. Seems to be a theme around here."

Seeing him look so sick forced me to come to the realization that he wouldn't have been capable of going to the cave and murdering Brandon. He barely looked healthy enough to stand behind desk. Carl was officially off my suspect list.

"Who did you hire?"

He gave me a suspicious look. "Why?"

"Well, obviously he may have done something to the car and someone like that sounds like trouble."

Carl let out a heavy sigh, his shoulders drooping as he raised his hands in a helpless shrug. His normally strong demeanor seemed to fade away, leaving him looking more vulnerable than ever. With a defeated slump, he leaned his weight against the sturdy desk.

"I believe in offering everyone a fair shot." And some people, they have reasons that they can't be official and all. He told me his name was Clay but I didn't get an ID or anything like that. Our plan was to give it a week and assess his performance. He didn't manage to stay for a whole week.

Mary arched an eyebrow. "So that probably wasn't his real name?"

"Probably not. Look, I'll check out your car. I'm sorry about all that. No charge and I'll do a little tune up too."

"Thank you," Mary said.

I tacked on, "Be careful." I was not at all sure if he should be working on anything.

"Ah, I can call my nephew up and see if he'll do some hours for me. He's got a much better job now but he's a good kid."

We thanked him and went out to the car where Lucy was waiting. I filled her in on the conversation.

"So Carl's out, but the suspicious Clay is now a new question mark?"

"As always, just adding more questions even when we do get answers."

Mary left the parking lot and headed to the bakery. I wasn't sure what Millie liked so I got an assorted box and then we were off to the dispatch station by the sheriff's office. I messaged Millie to let her know we were there.

Millie came out, smiling in the early sun doing the gimme-gimme grab hands at the doughnut box. I laughed and handed them over. Mary and Lucy, along with me, followed her down the sidewalk to a shaded picnic area in the back.

"This is usually the smoke break spot but there's only one or two of them that do now so it stays pretty vacant."

"I would always be coming out here for breaks." I said, looking up through the tree branches high above us as the pale sunlight diffused through making them look like they were glowing.

"I do on occasion. It is a nice getaway from the ringing phones, computer screens, and bright lights." She said, before taking a larger bite than I would have expected, from a chocolate glazed donut.

Mary was already chowing down on the maple creams she had insisted on. Lucy had one too.

"Well, we think the robbery at the gold mine had something do with it. And possibly some guy who owns a blue sports car and may have also recently needed a gardener."

I realized how irrational I must have sounded, but Millie merely raised her brows. She finished her bite, including licking her fingers, before exclaiming, "How on earth did you get all that?"

I ran back down the list of incidents, coincidences, and evidence we had come across.

"Whoever it was, they were able to let some paperwork slide at a place where it would be highly monitored. They also probably stored the gold in that cave, which is what Brandon overheard somehow at work and wanted to find."

"We thought that Carl dude at Highlands was involved, since Brandon owed him money. And he has a blue sports car. But, today he said he had appendicitis. And let me tell you, that explains a lot about how he has looked this whole time."

"Hmm," Millie took another bite. I picked at a cinnamon sprinkled donut. "Oh! The rope, it wasn't red or new. It was one of those old tan ones, fiber-like." She nodded when my mouth fell open. "I told the detective what you said and it got him scratching his head. You know, you keep this up and I can get you an application for the department."

"Seriously!" I gasped.

"It might not be as serious as it seems. Perhaps he had two ropes."

"That's true," I said, thoughtfully. "I'm not trying to be a bother with all these questions."

"Well, I'm glad Brandon has someone fighting for him. Honestly, I snuck a peek at the files. They have the death as undetermined so the coroner isn't totally convinced it was an accident. Which is why there is a file now."

A huge breath of relief escape me. At least they were looking into it. I had begun to think I was going a bit nuts with my theories and that it had been an accident I just wasn't accepting.

"I can tell all of this to the detective, but I'm telling you now, he'll want to talk to you." Millie explained.

"I figure that will be happening soon anyway." I said. Mary nodded.

"Well, thats all I have currently. Not that I don't enjoy being fed and I don't mind helping out, but maybe we can chill sometime with a more relaxing reason." Millie said. She smiled. "But until then, I will do what I can."

"Thank you so much, Millie, and that would be great. I do feel guilty using you like this."

She waved what was left of her second donut as she walked away. "I'm not complaining!"

We finished up our own pastries before heading out. I left the rest of the donuts at the front desk of the sheriff's office with the antisocial and attitude abundant receptionist.

CHAPTER 16

"So, now what?" Lucy asked. She'd taken the back seat for the ride back, for which I was grateful. Motion sickness hit me bad in the back seat, and I didn't want to see that doughnut again.

I thought for a moment. The thought of Hank and that shiny pendant all tangled up came to mind. The cat's gift from Mr. Thornberry. Which reminded me of Mr. Thornberry's professed love for antiques. "What do you think about going back to that antique store?"

"We visited it already. They said they hadn't hired him."

"We know Brandon was interested in it. Otherwise why would he underline it on his list to stand out?"

"Why would he care about it?"

"I'm not sure," I confessed. But I wasn't thinking clearly that day to really ask good questions." I know I sounded doubtful.

"What if he was looking into the gold there. Sell it off or something," Mary offered.

"He didn't steal the gold," I said adamantly.

Lucy piped up then, "Besides, I don't think antique shops buy gold. I thought only pawn shops did. If a large quantity of gold dust got stolen, wouldn't people start searching for it? Like the police?"

"Well, gold *is* super easy to melt because it's so soft."

I must have given her a surprised look, because Mary laughed, "I watch science stuff sometimes, it isn't always rom-coms and thrillers."

I nodded. "I think you're right. They probably smelted it right away. Turned the gold into bars, and then into jewelry they could sell anytime and anywhere. There would be no way it could tie them to the robbery."

Mary pointed. "See? Now who's watching the science stuff?"

"Actually detective stuff," I corrected. "It was in the last book we read for book club."

"Oh, yeah! You're right!" Lucy exclaimed. "Jessie recommended that one."

"It was good," I admitted.

"All right, then. Just a little side trip before we go home."

We arrived at the quaint antique store and stepped through its creaking doors. The tinkling of a small brass bell greeted our ears as Betty, wearing a warm smile, waved from her post behind the polished counter. The air inside was filled with the faint scent of aged wood and musty nostalgia.

Once again, uncertain of our quest, we wandered the cluttered aisles, hoping to stumble upon a hidden treasure that would offer a subtle clue or whisper of guidance.

I checked out the jewelry counter and only spotted antique baubles. Pins, clip-on earrings, and antique rings. Nothing that spoke of newly-smelted gold.

On the way back to the entrance I spotted a toy Pillsbury Dough boy high on a shelf. When I was a kid, I had one just like him, and remembered hours playing outside with him in the mud, making pies. I had to have him, and stood on tip-toes to scoop him up.

"You found a little treasure," Betty said as she wrapped him.

"I sure did." I accepted the package, and we wished Betty a good day and exited the building.

On our way back to Mary's car, I happened to glance upwards.

My eyes caught the sign hanging above the entrance. The name of the shop was elegantly painted, its bold letters contrasting against the weathered wood. Suspended from the sign was an actual antique red door, the same one that had clued Marguerite in when we first told her. It's worn paint telling stories of years gone by. My gaze was drawn to the brass arrow in the center of the door, its polished surface catching the sunlight. It pointed left.

Mary muttered as she jammed the key into the ignition, "This red door should be it. I don't understand."

"Do you guys see that?" I pointed.

"What?"

"There's an arrow on the sign. What do you think? Could it mean what we read at Brandon's house? Follow the arrow?"

Mary turned to me with a grin. The one she usually gave when she had the winning hand at cards. "There was an arrow by his note. I think this is it."

"So, we go follow it, then?"

Lucy made the decision for us. "Absolutely!"

"Absolutely sounds great, but we only have a short time before we have to get back to the manor. Cook said she can't cover for us again."

"Fingers crossed we'll see something within the next few minutes that makes sense." Mary put the car in gear while Lucy struggled to get her seatbelt on.

The narrow road unfolded before us, its worn surface bumpy and strewn with potholes. The once distinct lines had faded away.

"Wow! Someone needs to trim the overgrowth around here," Mary said and then glanced at me. "Do you think this is the job he was hired to do?"

I shook my head. "No. The county takes care of everything all this along the road. Besides that, the pruner he was looking at was for really tall trees."

Mary continued to drive, her hands gripping the worn steering wheel as she leaned down. Her eyes narrowed as she peered through the smudged windshield.

It was hard to see anything. Hidden driveways were betrayed by rusted mailboxes to signal quick glimpses. The few houses I saw appeared aged with weathered exteriors. Their peeling paint revealing years of neglect. A sense of abandonment lingered in the air, as if the houses themselves were whispering forgotten memories.

Just when I was about to give up, a blur of blue came hurdling half in our lane toward us.

I squealed. Mary quickly moved the car to the side of the road. Adrenaline shot through me as she drove as close to the edge as possible to get out of the way.

The wind rocked us as the sporty speeder rocketed past. I spun around in my seat to stare at the car. It quickly disappeared around the bend so fast I couldn't make out a thing.

"Did you see that? He nearly killed us! Is he brave or stupid with the size of some of these potholes?"

"Stupid, for many reasons. Hopefully, he learns to keep it in his lane before he gets someone hurt. Or worse."

The road appeared to stretch on for quite a while. I spotted several roads further down the slope that disappeared into the trees, but nothing stood out.

"I guess we should just head back." I said, reluctantly. "We need to pick up Cook's car anyway."

Mary agreed and turned back to the Highland's Garage.

A short time later, we were back at the dusty parking lot. Cook's car was parked over by the end of the building, so I figured that meant Carl had gotten around to it.

"I'll go grab the keys and meet you at the manor," I told Mary and waved goodbye. They'd already pulled back out onto the road as I went in.

"Keys are on the counter." Carl grumbled as I walked through the door.

"What was wrong with it?" I asked, noting his mood had definitely worsened.

"Some loose plugs. It's all good to go now. I think that moron just made a mess and didn't know how to put things back together right."

"Okay, well thank you and I hope you get to feeling better."

Carl gave me the tiniest of uplifts at the corner of his mouth with his nod. I felt like I had made a huge step with the ornery older man. It was almost a hint of a smile. I bit my lip to hide my own grin. I was baby-stepping my way into the hearts of the close-knitted town folk. Seeing him grimace made so much more sense now that I knew he'd had surgery. Why do people lie about even the simplest things?

It only took us a few minutes to get to the manor. I parked around the massive garage next to Mary's car and headed around back on the bricked path to the kitchen entrance.

The scent of herbs, beeswax, and flowers filled the air.

"Hello, dears!" Cook called from behind the kitchen table. It was lined with stacked piles of folded clothing. Marguerite sat in a chair with a needle and a thread. She licked the thread and, squinting, poked it through the needle.

"Hello," I said and handed over the keys. "Carl apologized. Apparently he had temporary help while healing from appendicitis and that one didn't pan out so well."

"I see, but it's good to go now?" she asked.

"Yep, and he even did a tune up. He said it was good for an older car to have one anyway."

"Pah, it's not old, just well loved for an extended period of time."

She looked up between the two of us. Marguerite continued to patch a tear in a pair of pants.

"Anything new?"

"Not really. I have a crazy theory."

"Can't wait to hear it."

I hesitated.

"Come on, spill it."

"Well, there is a possibility that gold may have been hidden in the cave. Maybe Brandon wanted to steal what was stolen." I winced before I even looked up, dreading to see the blatant, "I told you so," in Marguerite's eyes.

Marguerite froze, her needle in the air.

"We thought of a possibility that a wealthy worker at the mine, someone who needed yard work and offered it. Millie said the broken rope was an old tan one. Brandon's was red and brand new."

"Well, I'll be," Cook said. Marguerite still said nothing.

Quickly, I continued. "I have these cigarette butts, a lighter, and the rope as proof someone else was there."

"What did the police say?"

"I haven't talked to them yet but Millie said they will want to talk to me soon if I keep finding these little things."

Marguerite nodded.

Cook snorted. "Well, at least they haven't come beating down the door and threatening to arrest you. I'd be going in after I gave them a piece of my mind."

I didn't laugh at her threat. I knew she'd be good for it.

We all went off to finish our evening chores. I was beginning to feel like I would never get any real answers, much less solve Brandon's murder.

CHAPTER 17

That night we had our usual cocoa time in my room. I was quieter than usual, which wasn't saying much because my energy left at night like I'd been unplugged.

Wearily, I lowered my head to the rim of my mug, and breathed in the sweet chocolatey steam.

"Laura Lee, I sense a darkness creeping into your thoughts," Mary said.

Her melodramatic comment made me snort. "Darkness? Really? What have you been watching?" I could only imagine what latest drama had been on her recent obsession.

Ignoring me, she plowed on. "Don't get discouraged. We don't have the resources and know-how of the police that are in on this. But, if we can tie this to that gold theft, the FEDS will get involved."

I nodded. It dawned on me that I still carried the belief that the world was pitted against me. Funny how that feeling crept in when my heart hurt. But that feeling led me to feeling like a victim, and I hated that. I was resilient, I was strong, and most of all, it wasn't true. I had Brandon's aunt, as well as Millie and Mary all on my side. I bet some of my questions roused more interest from other people around town, as well.

I sat up straighter and tried to be more determined. "I wish there was an easy way to connect the bullion robbery to his death. I'm sure they'd take it so much more seriously."

"Have a little hope, right? So cheer up, buttercup." Mary groaned and covered her eyes. She shook her head. "I can't believe I just said that. What a thing to say. I'm sorry. None of this is cheerful."

"I knew what you meant."

"I'm confused about the car thing, though," she said. "Help me make sense of this. We know Brandon had a cool car. The garage guy has a blue car, but it isn't the one we are looking for. Then there is this mention of a Datsun which got a ticket near where the cave is shortly after the death."

"Yes, that's right, as bananas as it sounds." I ran through all the information I could remember. Since I wasn't into cars, it was difficult for me to keep track of the makes and models. "I think that's about it."

"So, I think that means our suspect is pretty wealthy."

"Or at least upper middle class," I interjected.

"Right. So he probably has a fancy yard that needs a lot of gardening that recently was done."

"Tall trees," I reminded her."

"Tall something." She grinned. "Drives a race car and worked at the mines?"

"I'm sure we can find him. We should also get a lottery ticket."

She grinned wryly. "I like our chances." She must have seen my face fall, because she quickly said, "Seriously, let's not lose hope. There is that car we saw near the Red Door antique place."

"The one that tried to kill us?"

"That one. And the arrow."

"I should just call Brandon's work friend, Kyle, again. Would it be so crazy if he knew who drove a sporty, blue car?"

I felt a bit embarrassed that I hadn't thought of it sooner. After all, it seemed really obvious. I pulled out my cell phone just as we entered the last turn leading to Thornberry Manor. I didn't know him very well, and hoped a text wouldn't be too out of the blue.

"I feel like a dork for not having thought of it sooner," I confessed.

"Hey, I'm the smart one of our detective team."

I laughed again.

"Okay, maybe we're equal there. Anyway, you've had a lot on your plate," she said kindly. "

I rolled my eyes and got out my phone. My fingers flying, I sent a quick text. **—Hi, This is Laura Lee. Quick question, do you know any of the higher ups at the mine that drives a blue sporty Datsun? A bit of a speeder?**

Kyle didn't message back right away, which crushed my hopes.

"All, right, well it's time for me to hit the hay," Janet said, getting up. Mary followed after her, both of the girls saying goodnight.

As the door shut, a sweet peace came into the room. I leaned over and set my mug down and shut off the light. Hank made a little brrrt noise from the foot of the bed to let me know he was settled and cozy.

"Good night, sweet boy," I said as I slid under the covers. My eyes adjusted to the dark as I focused at the usual crack in the ceiling.

What if the garage guy had run into Brandon?

My brain played at the whole scenario of Carl running across Brandon and chopping the rope. But what about the appendicitis? Would he have sent his so-called apprentice to do the job? And how could that have helped him collect his money?

Somehow, despite these anxious thoughts that drifted into impossible high school tests, I fell asleep.

***

The next day was a bit slower. Marguerite had a request from Miss Janice for a few baby white roses for her breakfast tray. She sent me out to search, a job I loved the most. I slowly wandered around the garden with a mix of anticipation and uncertainty. The tranquil surroundings gave me a bit of peace that I craved since the funeral, a quietness that only green living things could bring.

I heard a noise by a bed of ferns and turned to look. Hank sat under a giant prehistoric looking plant, and blinked pleased golden eyes at me.

"Hey, buddy."

I held out my hand to tempt him, but he ignored me and turned away, apparently fascinated by a dandelion.

"Stinker," I said and sat down by him. His fur was soft and warm, the trimmed grass and moss cool. He rewarded my stroke with a rub of his cheek against my hand.

I couldn't help my smile. Bees happily went about their morning as if happy to be awake, dancing into and among the purple, blue, yellow, and pink petaled heads that peppered the rich, green grass of the garden. Through the trees I could see the top of the little house way in the background. That's where Stephen, the gardener lived with his little sister.

"Glory be!" I heard a gasp behind me. I turned to see Cook staggering back with her hand on her chest. "You scared me, hiding down like that!"

I jumped as well. She had scared me more than her, I was certain. "Oh, I'm sorry!" I said, climbing to my feet.

"What are you doing there?" she asked.

I was about to go into the tale when my cell phone buzzed.

Wiggling a bit, I pulled it out of my pocket and checked the message.

Kyle had written me back. He must have seen it when he woke this morning.

"I just need to clip these roses for Marguerite," I explained, and snipped a few from the white tea bush. Then I ran inside the manor, clutching the fragile stems. I had to find Mary.

Inside, the scent of freshly baked bread and fresh-cut roses wafted through the air, mingling with the earthy aroma of the herbs.

I found her tying her apron. She had breakfast service to arrange before her on the silver tray.

"Mary! Kyle texted back!"

"Hurry up and read it!" she said.

I read the message out loud to Mary. **—The only one I know of is the guy, Alan.**

I stared at her. "You think this is it?"

"I'm not sure. Don't you think it's a bit convenient?"

I knew she didn't trust Kyle. "I'm not sure. Let me text him back."

"Be careful. It sounds kinda of suspicious to me."

I nodded. I wrote back. **—Okay, thanks! Oh do you know where he lives? This Alan guy?**

I barely had time to get the roses in the wee vase and on the tray when his reply came in.

—No clue except him complaining about the roads over near Alan's house).

I typed back. **—Thank you so much again!**

He sent a thumbs up emoji.

"I don't know what to think. " I said to Mary, showing her the message.

Her eyebrows raised and she seemed more impressed. "Isn't that the road we were on earlier?" she asked.

"You're right! Maybe this is the guy?"

Mary shrugged. "I don't trust him. However, he does line up with the facts we know. Now, we just need to know if this Alan guy smokes."

"Yeah?"

"Because if he does, and it's the same brand as the butt you found, that might prove he was at the cave at some point."

I bit my lip, thoughtfully. It seemed kind of weak. Probably a lot of people smoked that brand.

She continued, "You have to just have a bit of faith. Can you imagine if we figure out he knew someone else who was there when you guys were?"

I nodded, trying to hide I still felt a bit discouraged. How would we figure that out?

"Plus." She held up one finger to indicate an important point. "We have to know how he pulled off the robbery. And is he still hanging around the gold mine?"

"Well, it would be very stupid and suspicious if he suddenly bolted right after the robbery had been discovered. He probably has to bide his time and make some legitimate reason for leaving."

Mary agreed. "Good point."

I gave her a quick hug. "Thank you so much for helping me."

She hugged me back. "Of course! That's what friends are for."

"All right, I'm going to take a minute before Marguerite sees I'm here and give a quick call to Millie."

"Go hide in the pantry. Let's get this figured out."

I snuck in and quickly dialed.

"Hello," she answered, sounding a bit bored.

"Hi, Millie. It's Laura Lee. I was wondering if you knew anything about a stolen blue sports car?"

"Hmm, on about that again, are we?" she asked, chuckling under her breath. "Well, I can tell you it was reported missing the day after Brandon died." She sighed, "And I can say that it might be the car that likes to collect speeding tickets around here. He can more than afford it."

"Alan something? Works at the the gold mill?"

"How did you...I swear, girl. We are gonna have to change your name to Sherlock or something."

"I prefer my actual name. It's after my grandma. But I will allow the occasional compliment," I replied.

She giggled, so I pressed on, hopefully, "You can't give me a last name, can you?"

Her response was quick. "I could but I doubt it will help and it would most definitely get me fired if the wrong people knew I did."

"Well thank you for confirming my other suspicions. I promise to hang out without it being about badgering you for information!"

Millie laughed. "I will hold you to that. Take care!"

I hung up and hurried to find Mary again. I had to tell her what I'd learned.

I found her in the parlor. I quickly grabbed a feather duster to look busy in case Marguerite found us. "So Alan sounds like he is definitely our guy. Now we just need to find proof to tie him to Brandon."

Mary said, "Of course, we will need to find him first. I just hope he doesn't skip town before then.

The breakfast bell rang then. Conversation would have to wait as we both ran for the kitchen to bring out the food.

CHAPTER 18

*H*alfway through cleaning the dinner dishes, with suds up to my elbows, a scary thought hit me. Someone knew we were in that cave.

It actually gave me chills to acknowledge it. How the heck had they known we would be there? How would I ever be able to find out who it was. Alan? Let alone prove it?

The longer I thought, the more perplexed I felt. There was no other vehicle nearby when we arrived, and the sound of the gunshot had been so bizarre.

I rinsed the pot and set it the strainer. Memories rolled through my head.

That horrible cave. That deranged gunshot. Where had it

come from? Had it been directed at us? Could I have narrowly missed dying that day?

Or had it been some hunter?

Millie had mentioned someone had gotten a ticket near there. Was it all just a coincidence? I knew the acoustics could have thrown us off. Maybe the shot had been fired from outside the cave, and the resulting echo gave the impression that someone was already inside.

I shook my head and scrubbed at the frying pan. Someone knew we were there *and* they showed up after we did. But how? Had it been some coincidence that they had driven by and spotted the vehicle?

Or maybe they had a camera out there. One of those battery-powered trail cameras.

I felt my pulse quicken. Could that be the answer? I needed to go back and check. One more trek down the slope. Third time was the charm, right?

Mary came by then. She grabbed a towel and picked up the clean pan. I filled her in with my latest theory as she dried.

Her brow scrunched in thought. "You really think the cameras will still be there? After the cops investigated?"

I, however was hot in my theory. I couldn't be dissuaded.

"Personally, I don't think they've done a great job, considering they think the rope broke."

"Have you thought about the possibility the person could still be monitoring the cameras?" Mary asked, briskly drying the pan.

"That is a possibility, I guess."

"Well, I'm coming with you."

"When can we get away from here, again? I asked, desperately.

She gave me a smug grin. "I just happen to know that Marguerite has volunteered us to help bring the clothing down to the hall where the charity event would be taking place. She is absolutely moaning about this charity, and insists it's just a way for people to clean their closets. She doesn't get why it all got dumped on the manor, but this is good for us. We can use Cook's car again, and go move the stuff from the dry cleaners to the event."

"When?" I asked, reaching for the last pot.

"Tomorrow."

***

We picked up the clothing from the dry cleaners. The crew smiled a lot and were super friendly as we started collecting the clothing. In fact, they helped to pile it in the car. Personally, I swear it was from straight relief that we were taking this mess away from them.

At the hotel, staff met us at the front doors. They had luggage racks ready for us, and quickly hung up the clothing. Once that was done, they whisked it away. I was impressed with their efficiency. It took us several trips, but soon all the clothing was transported to their event room. Tomorrow was the big day.

"All right, let's go," Mary said, relieved.

I glanced at the time. We had a bit before we had to get back. "You ready for this?"

"More than ready." With a cheeky grin, she pulled out a new rope from under her seat.

"For the hill? What would I do without you?" I said.

She shrugged. "Probably fall down the hill and die."

"Mary!"

A half hour later she pulled up to the guardrail. I felt my stomach tighten.

I was surprised to see there was still a large pile of stuffed animals, cards, puddles of wax from candles and other tributes at the guardrail. It was odd because there hadn't been a huge turn out at his funeral but there seemed to be a lot of people that wanted to memorialize him...or at least the place where he had died.

Glancing around, I checked out our surroundings. It was quiet. There were no sounds of approaching cars. I fastened the rope to the guardrail using a triple granny knot.

"You know what you're doing?" Mary asked, showing her first glimmer of fear.

"Sure," I lied as I gave the knot a test.

She didn't believe me. "You're sure this is safe?"

Of course, I understood her trepidation, given what happened to Brandon. Hadn't I felt the same way myself when I first went down?

"I promise it's not as steep as it looks. In just a few minutes, you'll see why I'm convinced it was murder." I slung my leg over the guardrail and started down the gravelly terrain.

She stared over the rail at me. "Did you have to bring up the "M" word right now?" she grumbled.

I made a show of how easy it was. "Come on down."

She groaned louder and followed me. We made our way carefully down the steep embankment to the cave below. The weeds had all recovered, like I'd noted on my last trip. I landed in a bed of ferns.

"Wow, you're right. It's not bad," Mary said, hitting the bottom soon after me. "You see the cameras?"

"Not yet. Maybe the person got paranoid with the investigation and took them down."

She dusted her hands off. "Well, let's find these puppies."

We headed straight for the trees nearest to the cave entrance. I saw the spot where I found Brandon's knife.

"Laura Lee!"

She pointed to a spot on the tree. I glanced up. A yellow plastic square sat in the scarred bark. It was obvious that something had been mounted on it.

"I think this may be a match to some of your other evidence." She nudged a cigarette butt on the ground with the toe of her shoe.

Grimacing, I bent down and saw it was the same brand as the other ones we had found. Broken branches surrounded the camera's previous location, prompting me to quickly scan the nearby trees. We quickly discovered that there were at least three locations with clear views of the cave entrance, and one higher up on a tree, facing the road.

"Well, someone definitely would have seen us coming if the camera was still there," I muttered. We scrutinized the last marred tree trunk and random cigarette butts at the base.

"You mean, this is how he saw Brandon that day."

I nodded. I took a few pictures with my phone of the places where the camera had been. Stepping to the side, I took some more images farther back so the angle could be understood. I took closeups of the cigarette butts too.

"Do you mind if I check out the cave again?" I asked. "Brandon and I had only got a little way in. I'm curious if there was something inside while we were going in. I also want to hear how the echoes are. Maybe you can holler or something?"

"Oh, that is some good thinking." Mary agreed.

The first step was to have Mary stay outside while I hurriedly made my way to the general area where I thought we had been. She enthusiastically clapped her hands in a cheerleader fashion. It sounded similar but not an exact match.

"Now, come into the cave a little," I said.

The second time she clapped sounded about right.

We tried her being at the end but it sounded all wrong so we went with the theory that he must have stepped just in side.

"All right, let's get out of here," I said.

"No way! I have no clue what we are looking for, but let's see what we find!"

"It's no good. I've checked the whole cave out already with Brandon's aunt. It just ends at a rock wall."

"Show me," she said in a chipper voice.

We used the flashlights on our phones as we walked to the end. It was just as unimpressed as the last time I'd been here.

"See," I said, limply gesturing.

"Wait..." Mary shown her light on a section at the bottom back corner. There were three rocks jutting from the wall.

She kneeled down and began to wiggle each stone. We both gasped when the largest middle one easily gave sway. Looking back at me in surprise, Mary wiggled the rock out and pulled it toward us. Sure enough there was a deeper cut out under where the rock had been and running a deep channel back into the wall behind the stones.

"Check this out," she pointed. "That's a security box."

"Open it!" I gasped.

"Can't." She tried to move it. "It's cemented in place." She leaned back on her heels to study it. "How did he secure it? Maybe with a rod through the cement?"

"Something for the police to find out," I said. I made sure to take more pictures on my phone. "To bad we don't have some simple easy DNA or smoking gun type of match going on though."

"Yeah, but we pretty much think we know who it is and know the basics, we just have to find something that brings it all together."

"Very true. I never thought I would have gotten this far as it is." I grinned. "Team Justice. Or something like that..." I muttered as Mary laughed.

CHAPTER 19

We were nearly back to the manor when I realized I had sand in my shoes. I could barely stand it, sitting there in the car. As soon as Mary parked back behind the separate garage, I opened my door and smacked it against the fender.

Mary beat me inside. I found her already talking to the head housekeeper.

"Did you get all the clothing over to the hotel?" Marguerite asked, as she folded a linen napkin from an enormous pile.

"All safe and at the hotel. Ready for the charity," Mary said.

"And your investigation? How did it go?" She added another crisp linen napkin to the stack.

"It went well. We're pretty sure one of the heads of the labs from the mine named Alan stole the gold. It's possible he may be the one who killed Brandon."

Marguerite paused. "Really? And why would he do that?"

"We think he thought Brandon found where he stashed the bullion. Killed him to silence him."

"My goodness."

"We think he might live past the Red Door Antiques."

She snapped another napkin into shape. "I remember you saying that."

"We just aren't sure where. Brandon had been planning to do some tree trimming down that way. You know, those tall trees? So that's our biggest clue," I summarized.

Cook sent me an impressed brow arch. "Oh, I know that area. On Conner road, perhaps? It's a bit past the antique store, but they have some decorative trees. In fact, I believe that's where they have the twenty-five foot primordial bushes."

Mary and I looked at each other. We hadn't seen that. Perhaps we just hadn't traveled far enough down the road.

"Sounds like another road trip," Mary said.

"Maybe we can finally get this guy," I said.

"Now, you girls be careful, though. I don't like the idea of you two snooping around a murderer's actual house." Marguerite tutted. "You make me worry, is all."

"Of course, we'll be careful."

"You both need to be down to earth. And I know just the chore for you."

Mary groaned, the sound expressing what was going on in my heart. Marguerite had a gift at assigning horrible chores.

Fortunately, this was not the case.

"Mary, I'd like you to go detail the morning room. And Laura Lee, please take care of the floors."

I have a confession. I really do love cleaning the floors. It's the one time I take off my shoes and slip around on the hardwood.

With another flip of a napkin, Marguerite dismissed us. We ran from the room to the closet down the hall from the Butler's pantry for cleaning supplies.

Mary grabbed a caddy, while I got together the floor cleaners. From there we separated, me to the water closet to fill the bucket, and her to the morning room.

I hauled the bucket to the front room and set it down. Hank

watched me from his sunning spot on the wide window sill. I went over to scratch his ear and give his chin a little tickle.

"All right, cutie pie. No paw prints on my clean floor."

He closed his eyes in a cat smile that he finished in a swish of his tail. Then he proceeded to ignore me with careful attention out the window.

I put my mop in the water and rung it with the little foot pedal. With clean lemon scent, I swiped the floor.

The top half had dried by the time I finished to the doorway. I glided across the gleaming floor as the sunlight danced through the front room's grand windows. My little sneak, Hank, had stealthily trailed behind me with his eyes fixed on the mesmerizing mop.

"What did I say, you little stinker. Did you mark up my floor?"

With his velvet paws, he delicately weaved between my legs, his tail moving like a pendulum. I loved his company, despite the few footprints I had to clean up. He added a touch of whimsy to any chore.

I went through the beautiful, spacious entry way and down the hallway. As we reached the majestic ballroom, its polished parquet floor beckoned us like a shimmering mirage.

Hank leaped over the floor like a graceful acrobat, his shadow dancing in the flickering candlelight.

Hank perched atop a regal pedestal and observed my progress with an air of satisfaction. His emerald eyes glimmered with mischief and pride, as if he knew that with his presence, even the most mundane task became a grand adventure.

***

That night, our little book club gathered in the little room behind Marguerite's bookshelf. The bookshelf itself was located in Marguerite's bedroom, and was just one of the many secret passages and rooms Mr. Thornsberry had developed in the Manor.

We settled on various chairs and sofas and sipped our tea. No pinkies were out, but a few cookies were dunked. I sat on the traditional red ottoman with Hank curled up on my lap.

I glanced around the room and my heart lifted, seeing how full it was with warmth and laughter.

Cook laughed, "Well now, ladies. This latest book—my goodness—quite scandalous! What did you think of the affair!

Marguerite huffed. "I should have known it was for hussy's, given it was your recommendation."

"Scandalous indeed, but it really defines the importance of discretion. A good lesson for anyone."

"Really, Cook!"

Jane giggled, while Cook simply lifted an eyebrow in mild response. "Well, Marguerite, I do believe you secretly enjoy these clandestine stories."

Mary piped in then with a look of innocence. "Marguerite. You might have a hidden passion for romance novels!"

Cook chuckled. "Marguerite with a secret passion? That's quite a thought."

Marguerite actually blushed. "Enough with your teasing! Let's focus on the book so we can get it over with and on to the next. It's my turn to pick. My brain has melted enough."

Lucy picked up a cookie. "Marguerite, what's the next thrilling novel you've chosen for us?"

The head housekeeper lifted her chin. "It's an intriguing mystery. A tale of secrets and betrayal."

We all did our fair share of oohs and ahh.

Mary snuggled into her chair. "Sounds exciting! I can't wait to get lost in it."

The air was thick with the scent of freshly brewed tea, its aromatic tendrils weaving a cloak of secrecy. Delicate porcelain cups clinked together, their contents swirling like dark secrets. Pages rustled as whispered conversations filled the room, mingling with the flickering candlelight.

Cook raised her teacup. "To secrets, mysteries, and this wonderful, secret book club of ours!"

We all raised our tea cups, toasting to their secret gatherings.

CHAPTER 20

I slipped out into the parlor where fresh roses had been delivered. From the gorgeous bouquet, I found a small white bud in the back and took it with a snip. I placed it in a crystal vase on the breakfast tray, and stood back to admire the finishing touch.

Perfect. Then, careful to not joggle the teapot lid, I approached the garden room with my softest steps. Miss Janice didn't like, as Marguerite worded it, all that horse clomping on the wood.

The sun streamed through the garden windows and cast a delicious warm glow over the elegant setting. Miss Janice, a woman of refined taste, enjoyed her breakfast in this serene room.

I didn't blame her. If I'd had the choice, I'd want to eat my toast and over-easy eggs here every day of my life.

The scent of freshly brewed coffee mixed with the sweet aroma of freshly baked fig and honey danish pastries.

"Good morning, Miss Janice. I hope you're having a good day," I greeted and carefully placed the tray before her. The silverware reflected a bit of sunlight.

Although she looked tired, she'd already applied her characteristic pink lipstick. Her eyes lit up as she surveyed her breakfast. "You remembered my rose. How lovely. Thank you." She took a delicate sip of orange juice from the crystal glass.

I smiled, pleased with her reaction, and dipped my head.

"The rose always reminds me of the Sunday breakfasts I had at my Gran's house in the summertime. She had the most lovely rose garden. And she made a mean Egg Benedict." Here, she touched the white rose with a soft smile. "Sweet memories."

"That sounds lovely."

She took another delicate sip of her juice, and I left her to enjoy her breakfast. I smiled, thinking maybe that memory made her morning a little bit brighter.

Once I felt safely out of her earshot, I clattered down the stairs. It earned me a disapproving squint from Butler.

Upon entering the kitchen I found Mary leaning against the counter eating a piece of toast.

"Good morning," I said, cheerfully.

She shoved the rest of the toast in her mouth and brushed her hands. "Guess what I did last night?" Her curls were in their usual uproar.

"What?"

"I took a little virtual drive on the internet down Conner Road."

Excitement shot through me. "What did you find?"

She ignored the question. "I looked for very tall trees, you know, the kind that may need to be pruned."

"What did you find?" I demanded again.

"I just kept scrolling down the lane. It's quite cute, you know. Homey for a rich neighborhood."

"Mary!" I yelled.

She grinned, satisfied. "I might have found it."

"You did!" I shrieked.

"Heaven help us," Cook muttered at my outburst.

"So then I wrote down the address and put it in the search bar. And here's the name that came up. Alan Corbin."

"Wow! Okay." I tried to process what that meant to us.

"That's not all. It also brought up a help-wanted site, with a big ol' add by the infamous Alan Corbin."

She'd done it. "You definitely found the match!" I yelled. I hopped up and ran over to hug Mary.

Cook looked on with grumpy eyebrows. "I appreciate the cheerleading, but if you ladies could please get to those dishes."

I hurried to the sink and started on the plates I found there. Mary made a fresh pot of coffee, mimicking my great show of being busy.

A short time later I grabbed a quick moment. Mary had sent me the posting. I read through the help wanted ad Alan had posted. He'd been looking for a landscaper, but that position had a black banner across it, saying "filled. He was looking for house cleaners to prep the home for an upcoming sale.

The information fit with our theory. Apparently, he had plans to leave town soon.

"I have the perfect plan," Mary said, when I caught up with her. " We can pose as housekeeping. Which means a phone call to get accepted, but that would probably be the safest route anyway. He wouldn't suspect us of anything. Even better, we can snoop around a bit."

"I love it. Make the call."

"Now?"

"Mary!"

She grinned, impudently, and made the call that night while I brushed my teeth.

"Alan Corbin?" she said brightly.

"Yes," A deep male voice rumbled over the speaker phone.

""Yes, hello, I'm calling about the help ad? Are you still looking for housekeeping?"

We planned to make the package deal of me and Mary more appealing, by offering an especially low price for the work. If he was who we thought, he'd be pinching pennies.

He agreed to it and the appointment was scheduled for the next afternoon. Perfect, because that was our day off.

"Are you nervous?" Mary asked after she hung up.

I nodded. "Beyond, actually."

"Me, too."

"What if he does recognize me? This is probably the guy who shot at us the day we were at the cave." A lump grew in my throat. Could I really do this? "This is the guy who probably murdered my poor Brandon. He didn't deserve that. He was a good guy, with so much to live for."

Mary gave me a big hug, her eyes brimming with tears.

"I know, honey. Now let's go see if we can get him put away for life for it."

CHAPTER 21

The next morning, we loaded up the cleaning supplies and dressed in jeans and similar light blue t-shirts and then headed out to Conner Road. Having an actual address helped get us directly to the gate in no time.

"We didn't get this far the other day," Mary said, pulling into the driveway.

I nodded and stared up at the house. The house was huge with faux river rock walls, and the yard appeared fully manicured. My gut clenched as I realized the trees were freshly trimmed, within the last few weeks. Brandon had been here.

Mary saw where I was staring and her brow arched. "You okay?"

My tongue dabbed my bottom lip, and I nodded.

I followed Mary as she lugged the cleaning basket from the trunk. She passed it to me, and we headed toward the dark stained, heavy wooden door. My body trembled, and I forced it to calm down.

Mary reached over and knocked. She whispered, "Remember, we are anonymous. Just Jane and Jill from the hills."

Well, that did it. My nerves turned into a choking laugh. I did my best to disguise it into a cough and put my professional face on. What had we gotten us into? And those names?

The door opened, and a short woman stood there. She wore a dark blue skirt suit, and had a rather turned-up nose. "I'm Rebecca Smith, the realtor. Alan said you would be coming by."

My eyebrows rose in surprise. I hadn't expected a realtor. I tried to cover, which meant I sounded like an idiot by reiterating the obvious, "Yes, we're here to clean the home."

"Good. Wonderful. Why don't you come in. He's out at the moment." She stepped back into a dark foyer to welcome us in.

"Oh, is he not here?" I asked, hoping it didn't sound weird. I'd really had assumed to at least clap my eyes on him.

"Mr. Corbin may be back before you two leave. Come in. I'll show you the house."

I briefly glanced at Mary. She subtly shrugged.

Readjusting my cleaning basket, we went inside with Rebecca. I tried my best to appear especially attentive to what she was saying. I wanted to avoid any suspicion.

"So, as you can see, it needs an overall clean." Her voice raised to match the snooty expression. "A property like this will naturally attract wealthier clients. They have high standards. Will you be able to meet them?"

She turned back to stare at us with icy blue eyes.

Mary piped up, "Of course. It's what we do for a living."

Rebecca raised an eyebrow. "Well, what would you do in this room." She gestured with a graceful hand.

Mary looked around. "Well, for instance, besides the obvious, all the trim needs to be wiped, and the corners vacuumed out." She flashed her best, winning smile.

Rebecca flicked her gaze toward me, to see if I'd measure up. It was strange how people could seem to be the nicest people. But, if they knew you cleaned houses, they treated you as if you were beneath them.

I gave her my best humble attitude. It must have reassured her because she continued the tour. We dutifully followed after her. She went room to room, pointing out the issues she was concerned with and the areas where she wanted special attention used to make it "perfect."

We came to a closed door. Rebecca paused, then shot us a deadly stare. "Except this room. No one is allowed in this room."

"Not even to clean?" I asked, immediately intrigued. I caught her curious expression and dampened my own.

"Not even for me to show it. Whoever buys it will have to understand that space is sight-unseen until they own it."

"Well, that's a little scary. It could be hiding anything. Bodies, even," Mary said.

"Don't be so morbid. It's where he keeps a few of his special antiques. He doesn't want any possible damage to come to them. Otherwise, it's a normal room. An office. Now, come along."

We walked back through the living room and into the kitchen. She walked over to the island, covered with paperwork. "If we can just discuss the pay rate."

Mary walked over with her. I glanced out the sliding glass door.

There was a garage in the back. The bushes here weren't nearly as manicured and grew up around the base. The overgrowth even crept up one of the walls and framed a window. I was trying to decide if it was blackberries or wild roses, when I noticed the grass had been matted down in front of the door. Matted down to the point that dirt showed through in a dusty stripe.

I glanced back at the window. A perfect little peek-point to check out the garage.

"What about that garage? The one way in the back?" I asked.

"Mr. Corbin plans to hire another groundskeeper to finish up the yard. After that, he will probably need that cleaned as well," she stated.

"I'd like to take a quick peek inside. It will help me plan what I need to bring to clean it," I said.

"Didn't you bring stuff?" She asked with a pointed look at the cleaning basket. Seeing her suspicious expression, I scrambled to come up with an excuse.

Luckily Mary beat me to it. "We have supplies for the house. But the garage might need things like concrete degreaser, and such. Those are things we wouldn't normally bring."

Rebecca nodded. "Of course. That makes sense. Well, I don't

recall the flooring, but Mr. Corbin does work on his project car out there. I suppose it couldn't hurt."

Mary came through with the win on that one.

We followed the realtor out the slider. I was rather impressed at her skill to navigate the brick patio in her high heels. Even the overgrowth didn't stop her, although she made high, exaggerated steps through the tall grass. Nerves brought the giggles back and I had to fight them down.

Soon we were all in the building beyond.

"Ah, yes. Here we are." She shot us her realtor's smile which quickly died away as she remembered who she was showing this too. "I hope he will let us clean this up. His first showing is next week. It would be nice to have it cleaned by then."

"Is he still living here?" I asked. "It's such a beautiful home."

"For a bit. Once we get a sale, he plans to leave the state. He says it can't happen soon enough."

I was surprised at the disclosure but happy to have the info. Hopefully, Mary and I could get what we needed to have the police out before then.

The agent unlocked the door. She reached along the wall to flip on the light switch. With an expert step, she moved aside so we could go ahead of her and look.

It took all the self-control I could muster not to react at the sight of the blue Datsun. The same sporty little race car that had blown past us before.

I think Mary felt the same way from the odd sound that came from her throat.

"You okay?" Rebecca asked, her eyes narrowing.

"Just dust." Mary smiled.

Casually, we proceeded to walk around as if giving the concrete floor a harsh study. We examined different parts of the garage and recommended strategies for cleaning.

The realtor seemed relieved that we were confident in cleaning the dirtiest area we had encountered so far.

I followed Mary to the back wall with a long work bench. It was then I noticed three odd-looking cameras. All bright yellow, and one with a cracked lens.

CHAPTER 22

*M*ary silently mouthed the words, "Trail cams."

I pressed my lips together with a quick nod and turned away. It took everything I had to act natural.

These camera's went far in confirming our assumptions. But my eyebrows nearly flew off my head when I saw an ashtray filled with cigarette butts. I quickly snagged one and dropped it into my pocket.

"We'll definitely need to get the nicotine tar off the walls," Mary said, acknowledging that she had seen what I'd grabbed. "Some primer, perhaps? In cement gray?"

"That would be wonderful." The realtor beamed.

I smiled back. "We sure appreciate you giving us a preview of the garage. It turns out, we are well-prepared. We can get this show-case ready for you in no time. You can count on us."

"That is a wonderful quality to have! I'm glad Mr. Corbin was able to get you guys in."

The three of us returned to the house. Rebecca disappeared into the dining room, while we put on quite the show of cleaning the entrance and the spacious living area beyond it. Over time, we became comfortable as if it were a genuine job.

A few hours later, Rebecca found us in the primary bedroom and bathroom. She gave the bedroom an anxious glance and then nodded.

"Here you ladies go," she said, and presented us with a check signed by the realty company with a blank spot for our names.

My eyebrows rose as I saw the amount. Wow! Much more than I expected, but I hadn't been paying attention to that part of the conversation. Perhaps Mary and I should consider starting a side-business.

Something, however, with legitimate clients, instead of suspects in a murder.

"So, I'll see you tomorrow for the garage, correct?" the agent asked. We agreed. She walked to the back of the house, her heels clicking.

Despite her promise, Mr. Corbin never did show up. Unable to delay any longer, we packed our stuff and left the house.

The sun had set to just below the freshly trimmed trees. It made my heart hurt to look at them. I carried the heavy basket to the car with sore hands.

"Laura Lee, over here." Mary whispered excitedly, her hand flapping like a frantic bird.

Leaning against a shed was a pruning saw, the same type I'd found reference to at Brandon's house. And on the handle, a *blue star*. Her eyes went big and she grabbed my arm. "Are you thinking what I'm thinking?"

"What?" I wouldn't wager on that bet. Her brain came up with all sorts of things.

"Let's go sneak around and try to see into that one room."

"The locked office." Instantly, I felt like a thief. I rose up into tip-toe mode.

"Stop it. Act casual," Mary said, shoving my shoulder.

She talked a big game, but I noticed she seemed up on her toes as well.

We edged around the house. Rebecca could be seen through the window seated at the dining table. Quickly, we ducked down. The agent's voice came through, and I held my breath to hear.

"Sounds like she's on a business call," Mary whispered.

I nodded. She spoke of some closing date, and something on the MLS.

We continued our crouch-walk under the window. At the corner, we scurried along, both of us trying to take care on the edging flowers.

One more corner, and we were here. Mary stopped under the office window, with me creeping up next to her.

She stood and took a peek. I waited, and held my breath. Other than birds and a light breeze, all was quiet.

Her hand reached in my direction with a waggle. "Give me your phone."

"Who are you calling?"

"Shh. Be quick. I need to take pictures."

I lifted it up and she rapidly snapped a few. A door slammed. She dropped to the ground with a pale face.

"Go, go, go," she whispered, shoving me forward. We crab-walked around the building again, keeping below the windows.

At the driveway, we ran to the car. When we got inside, we both started talking, each over the top of the other.

"Both the car and the exact trimmer Brandon got were present."

"Plus the cameras and cigarette butts." She started the car and backed out.

"That last bit sounds more nefarious than it should," I said with a giggle. "What was in the locked office?"

"Look at the pictures!" Tires spinning in the gravel, she turned onto the road.

I rocked a bit in my seat. I opened up the album and started to scroll. Sparkles met my eyes. "Wow! It's jewelry. Lots of jewelry."

She nodded. "The place had more than Tiffany's"

"Just look at all that gold." I was mesmerized.

"We should head straight to the police station," Mary said.

I messaged Millie and told her we were coming and that I had a lot to tell her. She sounded relieved I was finally going to talk to the police.

No more relieved than I was to finally have something to share.

I leaned back in the seat with a smile. "Brandon, this is for you," I whispered.

"What?" Mary asked, her eyes on the road.

"Thank you for coming with me," I said.

"Just shut up. That's what friends are for."

CHAPTER 23

*A*fter we left the house, we were starving, so we made a quick stop at the drive-the through. The burgers helped a lot, I have to admit.

At the police station, I was sad to see that the receptionist was the same one from months prior. She hadn't sweetened a bit since our last encounter.

Her brow wrinkled when I approached, and she announced rather dourly that the investigator was already waiting for us.

Millie truly had paved the way for us.

A large man came right out to greet us before we had a chance to sit down. "Ladies! Welcome." He held the door open. "Come in, come in. I'm Detective Cash. Millie said you guys had some information for us? Something about the gold theft?"

Surprise hit me when he said that. Shouldn't the focus be on Brandon's murder? They really seemed stuck on the idea that he had an accident. Would the detective believe what I had to say?

"And a murder, yes." I said bluntly.

His smile disappeared. "This way, please."

We followed him down the stinky hallway and into his office. He gestured to two folding chairs. Nervously, I pulled one out and sat down. Mary did the same.

"Well, ladies?" He sat across from us and folded his hands on the desk top.

"First, there's this." I reached into my pocket for the cigarette butts I'd found. Then I gave him the one I'd found at the cave.

"This doesn't really help us since your fingerprints are all over them. Not to mention you moved it from the scene of Brandon's supposed murder."

I swallowed. This wasn't going well. Carefully, I pulled the lighter from my pocket and turned it over. He didn't seem impressed, until *Mary piped up with the explanation from the engraver.*

Still no real interest from Detective Cash. I felt like I was babbling as I told him that we had taken pictures. Mary nodded. "Yes! Laura Lee, show him your phone."

I passed it over. The detective told me where to send the photos I had taken.

"How did this guy come up on your radar in the first place?" He asked as he scrolled through them. He paused at one and zoomed in on the gold.

"The day Brandon and I went down to the cave, a blue car was spotted. We heard a rumor he got a ticket." I swallowed as grief welled up inside. I didn't mention Millie, not wanting to out her.

Mary took over for me. "We saw it in the garage in the back of Alan Corbin's house. He also has the tree trimmer Brandon bought. Brandon always put blue stars on his equipment, and it was on the handle. Also, we saw some of the trail cams. We suspect they were the ones we saw around the cave."

"Trail cams?" His eyebrow lifted.

"I saw them down at the cave the day we went," I said, defensively.

"How would you possibly be able to tell if they were the same cameras as the ones at the cave?"

CEECEE JAMES

"Easy. They were yellow, same as the bases that were left screwed in on the trees around the cave."

"Anything else?"

I swallowed. "One was bashed on the lens from where Brandon threw a rock at it."

The detective diligently scribbled in his notepad. The sound of his pen scratching against the paper filling the room. We recounted our theories, describing every minute detail we had uncovered. The process took much longer than I had anticipated.

"You sure you aren't ready to put an application in as a detective?" He smirked. "After how you helped my predecessor's case a few months ago, it seems you could be a regular Nancy Drew around here."

"No, thank you. I think I'll stick with housekeeping at the Manor," I said with a grin.

Mary and I finally departed, embarking on our journey back to our humble abode. The radiant setting sunlight cast a warm golden hue upon the landscape. We cruised along. I could hear the gentle hum of the engine and the faint rustling of leaves carried by a light breeze. The air was tinged with the scent of freshly cut grass and the promise of an approaching evening.

"Well, it's in their hands now." Mary sighed, her voice filled with a sense of relinquishment. We continued our homeward drive.

CHAPTER 24

We sat around the kitchen table, enjoying a quick cup of tea and snacking on homemade honey cakes. Mary was on her third. The amount of food she put away so fast always baffled me. As she ate, she finished the story to an eager audience around the table.

"So the cops got a search warrant and grab the cameras that day. One of the cameras showed footage with Alan on it. It was much worse than simply cutting a rope. He sprung out behind a tree and hit poor Brandon as Brandon descended with his back to him. The video showed him studying the rope. He tried to cut it, but the tensile strength proved to be as tough as Brandon had said." Here she pointed at me.

"I knew something was wrong when they said that rope had broke. It turned out, Alan also had a drive cam, which the police impounded. This camera showed how Alan pulled the red rope up and tossed it into his trunk. After scrounging a bit, he finally discovered a tan rope. This he quickly fastened to the railing, before cutting rope."

Mary jumped in again. "The end story turned out to prove Alan and his business partner stole the gold dust. Dust doesn't sound like much, but it amounted to eight million dollars over the past year. They stashed it in the cave behind a false back, and thought they were extra safe with the cameras to watch over it. No one knew about the cave, and they had no worries. They had no idea that Brandon had overheard about the gold in the cave after pruning the trees outside the window leading to Alan's private room."

"And they hadn't connected the stolen gold and Brandon before?" Marguerite asked. Cook watched suspiciously from where she was rolling out bread dough.

"Nope. But the rope that supposedly broke on Brandon was found to have gold dust on it, it became clear."

I nodded. "Now he has to decide if he wants to admit to murder to get out of the federal theft charges or admit to federal theft charges to get out of the murder. Not that it matters. Detective Collins said that everything I gave them laid the perfect path to all the evidence they needed."

"Did you girls get paid for the house cleaning?" Cook asked, with a bit of a smirk. "Because that's really the most important."

"I don't see why you care," Marguerite huffed. "You got your oil changed for free."

Mary's eyebrows raised in a fake offended expression. "Cook, who do you think I am? Of course we got paid."

"Just for the one day," I added.

Mary shrugged and took another bite. "And I bet she would have called us for more jobs if not for the whole deception part."

"Just a tiny bit of deception." I grinned, holding my fingers apart.

"Well, my goodness. All finished and just in time for us to host the charity meeting."

"I thought that was held at the hotel?" I asked.

"Of course, it is. However, the board meeting will be here, before the dinner. And, heaven help us, Miss Janice is in a tizzy because the Governor will be here."

"The Governor will be here?" I asked. "I can see why she wants to impress him."

"Oh, she does't care about about him. It's his wife, Harriet. Last year, you should have seen what she said about Miss Janice in the press. Miss Janice is out to redeem herself. Now, let's go ladies. Time to finish our chores. We have a long day ahead of us, tomorrow." Then, privately, she turned to me. "Go get the vase from the library. Careful, now. Miss Janice wants it out because it makes Harriet green with jealousy."

We all filed out to our assignments. I walked into the library, my favorite room, and found the item Marguerite had asked for. It was a bit nerve wracking to pick it up and carry it, but I still smiled. One of Mr. Thornsberry's antiques, and a big part of how we figured out the clue of the red door.

Carefully, I brought it out to the foyer, where Butler whisked it away from me in white gloved hands. The sun set low, the light drifting through the windows. Soon it would be time to serve Miss Janice her dinner, and then finish our evening tasks. I felt a sense of relief followed by the sadness that I hadn't fully grieved for Brandon. But I proved that he'd been murdered and I made sure that guy paid. Truth be told, that helped me deal with the loss a lot better than I would have thought.

Maybe this would bring his mother, Bertie, and Irene, his aunt, some comfort as well. Justice wouldn't bring Brandon back, but it did lift a bit of burden by bringing understanding.

It made me feel like I'd done something as well.

Tonight, I would write Bertie a card. I hadn't been able to talk to her that day at her house. I hadn't known what to say in the face of such terrible grief. But now, maybe I could.

Maybe not. The more I thought of it, the more insecure I felt. I didn't know what I'd say. There weren't any words that would touch her pain, and so far, everything that came to mind sounded stupid and trite. How could I possibly offer anything to Bertie?

I thought of my friends. Marguerite, Mary, Cook. Even Butler. It was through their compassion, love, and empathy that I experienced some comfort.

The more I thought about it, the simpler I realized my message could be. There were no right words, no right formula. Nothing could bring her son back or take away her pain. But at least I could let her know I cared. That I was here. That she was free to feel however she wanted and I would listen, if she wanted that. Some things could be too hard to talk about. I got it.

Brandon's life, and death had an impact on me, one that would touch me for the rest of my life. Among other things, it made me think of my own legacy and the mark I wanted to leave behind, and who I really wanted to be. To appreciate the beautiful things in life, and live by the same hope my Grandma taught me, starting with the Lord's prayer. I felt a lot older since he'd died, and I didn't know if I'd ever see that innocent Laura Lee again.

But maybe I'd come to like this new one even more.

The grandfather clock struck; time for dinner. I came out of my deep thoughts to see the sun had finally set, and a cool gray light filled the foyer.

"Laura Lee? Where are you?" Marguerite called me to dinner service. I turned to run for the kitchen, this time holding a grateful thought in my heart.

AFTERWORD

*T*hank you for reading the final book in the six book Secret Library series. I hope enjoyed Laura Lee and the Thornberry Manor as much as I did.

Tune in to the latest in the Baker Street Cozy Mystery series!

And if you like a nice, long series. Flamingo Realty Mysteries has 14 books and counting∼

Made in the USA
Monee, IL
11 November 2024

69872260R00128